TANGLED UP IN ICE

CHARLOTTE BYRD

D1522437

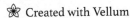 Created with Vellum

I have debts to pay and secrets to keep. When someone threatens my life, I crash into him: Jackson Ludlow

The recluse billionaire of New York

Once, he had everything a man could want. Then, he lost the only thing that he ever loved.

So, he spent four years holed up in his mansion doing the only thing he knew how to do:
make money.

We are all wrong for each other. He's cold, uninterested and demanding.

I'm impatient and inexperienced.

The only thing we have in common is that **we both have secrets.**

And the closer we get, the more they threaten to destroy us.

"Fast-paced, dark, addictive, and compelling" - Amazon Reviewer ★★★★★

"Hot, steamy, and a great storyline." - Christine Reese ★★★★★

"My oh my....Charlotte has made me a fan for life." - JJ, Amazon Reviewer ★★★★★

"The tension and chemistry is at five alarm level." - Sharon, Amazon reviewer ★★★★★

"Hot, sexy, intriguing journey of Elli and Mr. Aiden Black. - Robin Langelier ★★★★★

"Wow. Just wow. Charlotte Byrd leaves me speechless and humble… It definitely kept me on the edge of my seat. Once you pick it up, you won't put it down." - Amazon Review ★★★★★

"Sexy, steamy and captivating!" - Charmaine, Amazon Reviewer ★★★★★

" Intrigue, lust, and great characters...what more could you ask for?!" - Dragonfly Lady ★★★★★

"An awesome book. Extremely entertaining, captivating and interesting sexy read. I could not put it down." - Kim F, Amazon Reviewer ★★★★★

"Just the absolute best story. Everything I like to read about and more. Such a great story I will read again and again. A keeper!!" - Wendy Ballard ★★★★★

"It had the perfect amount of twists and turns. I instantaneously bonded with the heroine and of course Mr. Black. YUM. It's sexy, it's sassy, it's steamy. It's everything." - Khardine Gray, Bestselling Romance Author ★★★★★

DON'T MISS OUT!

Want to be the first to know about my upcoming sales, new releases and exclusive giveaways?

Sign up for my Newsletter and join my Reader Club!

Bonus Points: Follow me on BookBub!

All books are available at ALL major retailers! If you can't find it, please email me at charlotte@charlotte-byrd.com

Black Series
Black Edge
Black Rules
Black Bounds
Black Contract
Black Limit

House of York Trilogy
House of York
Crown of York
Throne of York

Standalone Novels

Debt

Offer

Unknown

Dressing Mr. Dalton

*H*er small, delicate mouth parts in the middle.

She licks her lower lip and my body burns for her. I lift my chin to hers. Our lips collide.

I bury my hands in her hair.

It's soft and damp with an earthy scent that doesn't come from any shampoo bottle.

She is soft and snug in my arms and she pulls away only far enough to utter, "I love you, too."

I clutch her closer, wrapping her arms around mine.

Her breaths become mine and mine become hers.

Her hands are ice.

She slips them under my shirt, and my back recoils for a moment before welcoming her in.

I'm restless and hungry for her.

All of her.

Right now.

That's what she does to me.

One touch and I have to have her.

Another touch and I morph into a beast who can't control his impulses.

With her chin tilted toward the ceiling, her long hair moves in waves.

I run my hands down the contours of her body. I know every curve and every dip.

The more I feel, the greedier I become.

CHAPTER 1 - JACKSON

HATE

I hate this city.

I hate the grime.

I hate the sad and angry faces that people make as they walk down the sidewalk.

I hate the rush.

I hate that everyone has somewhere more important to be than the person next to them.

I hate the way the poor kids from the projects look at rich kids with personal drivers.

And I hate the way kids with drivers look at everyone else, like they are specks of dirt beneath their feet.

I hate that a family of five has to cram into a one-bedroom apartment and pay two-thirds of their income in rent for the luxury of a two hour commute.

I hate that I live alone in a twelve thousand square foot, five-story mansion with a view of Central Park from practically every window.

I hate the summers with their hordes of tourists taking pictures of every mundane and uninteresting thing.

I hate the fall and the spring, with its torrential rains which chill you to the bone and make the city gray and gloomy for weeks.

But most of all, I hate those five weeks between Thanksgiving and New Year's that everyone else seems to find so magical.

It's the time of year that people spend hours gawking at window displays designed to dazzle and make you forget that you really can't afford anything there.

I hate the blinding lights that twinkle all day and all night without a moment's peace. But mostly I hate the cheer that fills the city, which only has one real purpose - to sell more crap.

I hate people and I hate that I'm alone.

I hate that I haven't left this house in almost four years and I hate how much I like being alone.

I hate that all I do is work, but without work, I'd have even less than I do now.

I hate my money, and I hate to imagine a world in which I don't have it.

But mostly I hate myself.

I hate the scars that cover my body.

I hate that every time I look at them, my mind is flooded with memories of *that* day.

I hate that the person I used to be is gone and I hate that I can't imagine my life without all of this hate.

CHAPTER 2 - HARLEY

LOVE

I love this city.

I love the lights that illuminate the streets until twilight.

I love that something is always going on.

I love that everyone is always in a hurry.

Where are they going?

What are they doing?

What is it that's so important?

I love the traffic jams and people honking when they are standing still.

I love how hot, steamy, and unbearable the summers get.

I love how everyone who has anywhere to go takes off for the Hamptons, Connecticut, Vermont, leaving the rest of us with a bit more room to stretch out.

The summers bring in all the tourists and I even love them.

I was one of those tourists once.

When I turned fourteen, my parents brought me here to show me the sights.

Statue of Liberty.

Broadway.

Times Square.

The typical places that all real New Yorkers avoid.

That's when I first fell in love with the city, and that's when I knew that I had to do everything in my power to move here.

And the thing that I love most is that magical time between Thanksgiving and New Year's.

The tree lighting ceremony in Rockefeller Center.

Ice skating in Central Park.

The storefronts and the lights that seem to explode with life.

But I also love this city on those other less lovable days; the cold, slushy days of February that are all too short.

I love the dirty snow that appears the day after a big blizzard, and I love the way there's always one rebel pizza place that remains open while the rest of the city closes down and everyone crams into it for a bite.

I love the crowds.

I *even* love my apartment.

And that's not easy to love.

It's a four-hundred square foot studio and I share it with a roommate.

Yet, I still love it.

I love the tiny kitchen in which every appliance is miniature.

I love the little closet, which only fits half of my clothes, and I don't even shop that much.

I love the little bathroom that has absolutely no space around the sink. I have to house the shampoo and conditioner in a wire hanger around the shower head and keep the rest of the products in boxes under the bed.

Why do I love this apartment?

I can't help it.

It's about the size of a large Barbie Dream House, if she had a Dream New York Apartment, but it's enough for me.

Maybe there's something more to all of this.

Maybe I love this place because of how it makes me feel about myself.

Despite what I have, or rather don't have, I feel important.

Special.

New York does that to people to get them to move here.

It's almost as if the city itself sends you these subliminal messages that say no matter how crappy your apartment is or how crowded, loud, and angry people are, you're in New York.

Just being here is enough!

That has to true, right?

Why would I love this place otherwise?

CHAPTER 3 - JACKSON

PRICE OF URBAN ELEGANCE...

a house is considered a mega-mansion by the real estate industry when it is over ten-thousand square feet.

Given the lack of space and the sheer number of people who live on this island, there are not that many mega-mansions around.

Even many hedge fund managers and some billionaires are forced to settle for six or seven thousand square foot apartments and buy bigger properties in the Hamptons, or Greenwich, to enjoy on weekends.

Though there isn't much room for many three-bedroom houses, let alone mega-mansions in the city, there was a time when the rich of New York were nearly as rich as they are now, adjusted for inflation, of course.

It was the turn of the century and the robber barons along with the bankers and other collectors of wealth built large homes overlooking Central Park.

Many of those homes were torn down or converted into multi-unit apartment buildings, but my house remained.

Somehow it has weathered the times and remained in possession of one wry widow who lived to the ripe old age of one hundred and two.

Unlike me, she had a big staff who also lived in the home, and like me, she also raised her child there.

I wouldn't admit it out loud, if pressed, but that's probably the main reason she sold me the house in the first place.

That and I had to sign a contract that said that I would never convert the place into "one of those horrid two-bedroom apartments for paupers they have littered this park with" - her words, not mine.

I am not in the real estate game and I bought this place solely because my daughter fell in love with it.

I would've paid thirty-five, and she would've

accepted twenty-five, but after some negotiation, we finally settled on thirty million.

And that was it.

The turn of the century mansion, with only one owner, and magnificent historic touches was ours.

Its *'limestone trim, broad, low stoops, and ionic porticos'* gave the mansion *'an impression of urbane elegance'* the listing said, but to us it simply became home.

After I made some updates, of course.

The team worked hard to incorporate many modern updates while maintaining the true character of the mansion, all for the bargain price of only five million.

When everything was finally done and we moved in, our bliss lasted only a short time.

Exactly eleven months and three days later, *it* happened.

Nothing was *ever* the same again.

PRICE OF COZY COMFORT

'Cozy' is one of those words that real estate agents use to describe small apartments.

It's a known fact.

But when I looked into living on my own, I realized that the types of apartments that were in my price range wouldn't even be described as cozy.

They'd have to use different words entirely.

They'd say, *'micro-loft'* if they really wanted to get the rental.

But if they wanted to be honest, they'd have to go with *'miniscule,'* *'tiny,'* maybe even *'illegal.'*

I know somebody who lives in a one-hundred square foot apartment with no windows or a bathroom door.

But it does have a mini-fridge and a hot plate with two burners.

I'm not sure whether the lack of a bathroom door is the biggest problem or maybe it's the lack of windows?

If I had lived there, I'd probably prefer a window because it's not like I would be hosting anyone for a visit anytime soon.

The renter got it for $1300 a month and was grateful because he no longer had to have a roommate or commute for hours each way from New Jersey.

The problem is that I can't even afford that on my own.

That's why I'm so grateful for Julie Debinsky.

Julie is from Staten Island and she doesn't have a trace of an accent.

Her dad had a refrigerator repair business that did well enough to send her and her brother to private school in Connecticut - hence the lack of accent.

"Those WASPS would've eaten me alive if they heard one nasal sound," she had said on a number of occasions.

Julie isn't honest with many people about her origins, but she is with me.

We both met at Columbia, or rather Barnard College. Barnard is located right across Broadway from Columbia, and it's the women-only college historically associated with the university.

Columbia didn't allow women to go there until 1983, but now all students are allowed to take classes in either place.

Most of my classes come from Columbia and my degree comes from Columbia University.

Despite how well we get along, if Julie's father was still married to her mother, I doubt that she and I would be roommates now.

But, when we were in our junior year, he left her mom for his long-time girlfriend, causing a big family rift.

Julie took her mother's side and her brother took his father's side.

That's why Julie lives with me and scrambles to pay $900 for her share of the rent and her brother lives in a two-bedroom in Chelsea and pays $8,000 a month.

My own situation is a bit different.

I grew up far away from here where the trees reach for the heavens and stay green year-round.

At home, properties of over an acre or more in space are not uncommon and most people have horses and a few dogs.

And then there are the mountains.

When the sun goes down, it bathes them in purple twilight, illuminating each ragged peak.

When I look out of my window onto the busy street below, I often think about all the space there is back home.

The sky is almost always blue, unless there's a big storm rolling in, and the clouds rarely hang low in the sky.

Everything is bigger and grander than it is here, at least when it comes to nature.

Don't get me wrong, Central Park is beautiful, majestic, and lovely.

But I find the fact that many New Yorkers think of it as *real* nature humorous.

I grew up in the suburbs of a pretty small city in comparison to the ones in the East, but it was one of the biggest in the state.

We lived in a three-bedroom, two-bath house on a nice street where little kids rode their bikes.

On the weekends in the winter we skied, and in the summers, we rented a house on the lake and went boating and swimming.

It was my parents dream to buy some land and

build their dream house, and slowly, over the years, their dream became a reality.

They bought five acres out in the country with a falling down farmhouse and an even more dilapidated barn.

Whatever extra money they had, they started putting into remodeling the place.

And by the time I was a junior in high school, it was ready.

Our new house had four-bedrooms, the master for my parents, one room each for us, and a guest room for visiting family members and friends.

In addition to a spacious kitchen and living room, it also had four bathrooms.

The entire house spanned close to three-thousand square feet.

Looking back, the day we officially moved in was the defining moment in my parents' lives.

They both grew up in small houses and had to share their rooms with multiple siblings.

When they bought their own place, the home that I was raised in, it was a big step up.

But it wasn't enough.

Their dream was to own *land*.

That's pretty much everyone's dream there in the

West, to own so much land that you don't see
another house for miles and miles.

The aim is to own so much land that it's just you,
your family, and the sky.

The big sky.

My parents were never wealthy.

But with a lot of saving and cutting back, they
paid a lot of their suburban house off when they
bought the land for the ranch.

They called it the Burke Ranch, after our
last name.

They finally sold the house when the Burke
Ranch was almost ready and paid down most of the
construction and renovation loans.

It helped that my father did most of the work
inside the house himself.

Up until I was in eighth grade, Dad always had a
second full-time job in the summers with the
forestry department because a teachers' pay is
hardly enough to support a family on, let alone big
dreams.

After Mom's promotion to Lieutenant with the
Montana Highway Patrol, she got a big raise, and
they decided that it would be better for Dad to
spend his summers off building the house.

The Burke Ranch took about six years to complete in total, counting from that impossibly cold and blizzardy February when they first went out to look at the land and paid almost all of their savings for it.

I think that I am only now starting to realize just how much of my childhood was consumed by their dream.

For two kids who were raised in subsidized housing and trailer parks, and shuffled among relatives with alcohol and drug problems, the Burke Ranch represented so much more than could be counted in monetary value.

They imagined it would be a place for them to grow old.

They imagined that this was where I would get married.

They imagined that this was where they would play with their grandchildren.

The Burke Ranch represented success in every possible way, including the beginning of a legacy.

But then it all fell apart.

CHAPTER 5 - JACKSON

LIFE AT HOME...

*I*n the mornings, I walk out onto the terrace off the master bedroom and look at the city below.

Up here, I'm somewhat safe from the pollution and the noise and I can breathe a little more easily.

I cinch my robe and sip from my cup of coffee.

It's morning to me, but the day is already in full swing for Manhattan below.

It's after nine and people are rushing around, scrambling, to get to the places they should've been already.

I am not a morning person and I prefer to sleep in until nine and start my day at a leisurely pace.

Given the fact that it's not unusual for me to

work until eleven at night, I allow myself this luxury and so do the people who work for me.

Clouds are hanging low in the sky, almost suffocating the city.

They are blocking the sun with their gray blanket, making the air thick with moisture.

I wouldn't go so far as to say that I enjoy days like these, but there is something appealing about them.

The gloomy darkness is a reflection of how I feel inside.

Yet, they come with a heaviness as well.

The sun, when it does peek through on those occasional winter days, does bring levity along with it.

It brightens my mood and gives me a kind of pep to my step.

Doing work suddenly becomes easier and sometimes, I even take a break and lay out on the lounger and sunbathe.

But today will not be one of those days.

A strong breeze comes up, bursting my robe open.

The cold rushes through my body and I turn to walk back inside.

I pick up a remote and flip on the fireplace.

Standing in front of it, I let myself warm up as I stare at my face in the mirror above the mantel.

The man I see there has tired eyes and olive skin.

My eyes are piercing blue and my jaw is sure and defined and is a perfect match to my strong Roman nose.

I look like I come from northern Italian ancestry, but in reality, I am a mix of Irish and Slovenian.

My grandparents, from both sides, were all immigrants just like everyone else in this country who weren't Native American or brought here in chains.

I tuck my hair behind my ear.

It's thick and dark and has grown a little too long and now falls in waves around my head.

I know I need to cut it again.

I haven't seen or talked to another person in the flesh in almost four years.

The advances in technology have made the transition to working from home quite easy and fluid, allowing me to interact with my employees entirely online via text and email, with only an occasional conference phone call.

Given the size of this place, I, of course, have staff who clean and take care of the pool and general gardening around the terrace.

But I avoid contact with them as well.

They all come on a rotating schedule that we have planned out ahead of time, cleaning parts of the house that I am not currently in.

The housekeepers, the gardeners, and the pool guy will all take care of the upper floors when I am downstairs.

If they need to come to my part of the house, they will text me and I will tell them which room to avoid.

The local grocery store delivers my standing order twice a week and if I want anything special from a particular restaurant, they deliver that as well.

Over the years, all the wrinkles in this system have been ironed out, allowing me total solitude.

I guess some people would be surprised that someone could live like a hermit in one of the largest cities in the world, but I find it quite easy.

The only real problem I ever run into is getting my hair cut.

You see, it's virtually impossible to avoid contact with another person if you need a haircut unless you do it yourself.

I head into my master bathroom.

There's a large clawfoot bathtub in the middle of the marbled floor.

I undress and step into the shower big enough for a party.

When I turn the knob and set the temperature, water comes out of all six nozzles at once, bathing me in warmth all over my body.

I welcome the change from the chilliness of the terrace, losing myself in the moment.

When I finally emerge, the room is warm and filled with steam.

I wipe the mirror with the hand towel and reach in the lower cupboard under the vanity for the professional scissors.

I brush my hair with a fine comb.

Holding a small section with one hand, in between my index and middle finger, I cut vertically, toward my hand like the hairdressers in the online videos instructed to do. When I'm done with one, I continue going around my head.

Then I toss my hair and look at the final job.

I purposely didn't cut it too short, just short enough to not fall into my face so much.

The job would be much better done by a professional, but overall, I am pleased with the final result.

It's messy and unkempt but lays as if it was meant to look like that.

I put away the scissors and clean the hairs off the vanity.

Then I return to the bedroom and the wide minimalist desk in the corner next to the sofa.

For work, I rarely need anything but my computer, so I find myself working a lot in here instead of my official office down the hall.

I like working here because it reminds me a lot of how I started out.

In a studio apartment, which was much smaller than this room, but had everything that I needed; a bed, a desk, a few bookshelves, and a computer.

It was the place that I started my empire and though this room is much more lavish and grand than my old home, working from this room gives me a bit of peace.

Of course, my tendency to avoid my office might also have something to do with what happened there.

CHAPTER 6 - JACKSON

WORK AT HOME...

As soon as memories start to flood my vision, I push them away.

If I let them linger too long, they will consume me.

So, instead, I open my laptop and look at the screen.

I check my email first because the requests and the updates from my employees and managers are the easiest way to keep the bad thoughts away.

Phillips sends me a proposal for three new podcast shows.

Podcasts are online audio shows that usually consist of one or two hosts who record their conversations on various topics and post the series on different platforms for others to listen.

They are popular with creators because they are relatively easy to put out and they are popular with listeners because they are free.

What separates good podcasts from the bad ones, however, is the content, the topic, and the vision of the creators.

The first clip that Phillips forwards me is a political one.

I'm not in the mood for current events so I put the political one aside and instead listen to the podcast from a psychologist offering marriage advice.

A woman calling into the show asks what she should do because she suspects her husband of infidelity and he is denying it. The wife isn't sure whom to believe - her husband or her gut.

The story is familiar and yet different, like all good stories are.

The psychologist expertly asks her for more details and I'm immediately drawn into her world. She advises her to trust her gut, but also to investigate further. To follow this advice is to follow a fine tightrope and I don't envy the caller at all.

As soon as I listen to the whole audition tape, I write Phillips back and tell her to buy the podcast.

Phillips is the Director of Operations at the Minetta Media Co., a company that I started seven years ago.

She is basically my number two and handles all of our acquisitions and operations.

Seven years ago, sitting at a cafe on Minetta Street in Greenwich Village, I had a lot of thoughts about different things going on in the world and I decided to channel that energy into a blog.

Unable to think of a good name, I went with The Minetta Blog as a placeholder.

While I had a lot of good ideas about what makes a good blog, I quickly realized I was much better at evaluating content and acquiring advertising than I was at actually writing.

So, I reached out to a few other bloggers whom I liked to read and brought them under my brand name in exchange for a share of the advertising money, which I didn't yet have.

They weren't making any money anyway, so they were eager to agree to my proposition.

Back then, I had two things going for me: lack of money and a whole lot of passion.

Oh, yeah, and not knowing a damn thing about starting a media company also helped.

If I had known how hard it would be to get it off the ground, to grow it where it is today, I doubt that I would've even tried.

Sometimes, ignorance is bliss.

After I got my first advertising contract with a small flower shop, which later became a national brand, I changed the name to Minetta Media Co., keeping the original Minetta as a tribute to where I'd started.

Now, Minetta is a media company that specializes in podcasts, blogs, and online articles about various topics, including in-depth analysis of current events and important world topics, as well as pop culture, and other lighter pieces.

When I first started, podcasts were still in their infancy and people were still trying to figure out what makes a good show.

But I loved this medium even more than blogs because it's so much easier to just listen to people talk about a particular topic than to sit down and read pages about it.

So, I started to invest in podcasts.

Most of the hosts were producing and putting out their shows for free, so they were only too happy to be asked to be a part of a media company that offered them a generous share of the advertising that appeared on their show without actually doing the work in acquiring those ad contracts.

Other media companies tend to use analytics and research firms in order to decide which direction to go in, but Minetta just uses me.

I stay on top of the trends.

I listen to a lot of different podcasts and read a variety of publications to see in which direction we might want to expand to next.

I figure I grew this company to an estimated value of one billion dollars relying on my judgement, so why change now?

The billion-dollar evaluation, isn't just Minetta, of course, not yet anyway.

Whatever profits I generated, I invested in various investment vehicles in order to keep Minetta afloat and, so far, it has worked out pretty well.

Scanning our lineup of podcasts, I suddenly realize that we still have very few focused on true crime. True crime is very popular with television magazine shows like Dateline and is a very fast-growing section of the podcast market.

I take out my phone and text Phillips.

.   .   .

WHERE ARE the true crime podcasts?

A MOMENT LATER, she responds.

I CAN GET you a list of contenders by this afternoon.

CHAPTER 7 - HARLEY

VANISHING OF DREAMS...

*L*ife is what happens *after*.

      We all have dreams and aspirations and goals, but life is what happens after we either achieve or fall short of whatever we imagine our life would be.

Life is what happens after the wedding.

Life is what happens after the move.

Life is what happens after we get the job.

In my case, life was what happened after the Burke Ranch went up in smoke.

One day it was there, and then it was gone.

Most of it, anyway.

Forest fires are a common occurrence in the West.

There's even a phrase that we use to refer to that time in the late summer and early fall when everything is still dry, but the snow hasn't come yet.

Fire Season.

Fires come and go, acres burn.

Some homes burn down, others are saved.

Most of the time, there is very little loss of life.

It was September and we had lived at the Burke Ranch just a little over a year.

The day started out just like any other.

The sky was bright blue without a single cloud around.

And then suddenly everything changed.

Even now, all of these years later, I can't take myself there.

I can't relive it.

I can't describe it.

It overwhelms me completely and if I let myself go there, then I can lose days in a depressing stupor.

What I can say is what happened after.

Life happened.

The state police and my father's school district held fundraisers, raising enough money for us to rent a two-bedroom apartment.

It was fully stocked with everything we would need, and our family will be forever grateful for this.

My parents filed an insurance claim for the ranch but were informed that my father had forgotten to pay one payment.

So, they technically didn't have insurance at the time when the fire happened, and the company denied their claim.

At first, my mother didn't blame my father and they decided to fight the company with a united front.

They hired a lawyer who took their case to court.

Months turned into two years and a trial, which they eventually lost.

And after that trial, everything fell apart.

If the fire insurance had paid out like it was supposed to, they would've received close to a million dollars, the real value of the Burke Ranch.

Since they still had the land, it would've been more than enough to rebuild.

But since their claim was denied, they had lost their retirement.

They had lost all the money that they had paid into their first house.

They lost all of that work that brought the value of the ranch to what it was at the time of the loss.

But the Burke Ranch wasn't the real reason they decided to part ways.

We all lost a lot more than just some property.

We lost *him*.

***

My brother was twelve years my junior.

He was a surprise baby and loved to pieces for it.

My parents tried to have more children after me for years to no avail, and then suddenly when my mom turned forty-four, she got pregnant.

They weren't using IVF or any other interventions because they couldn't afford them, and they'd pretty much settled on the idea of just having me.

And then Aspen came along.

Sweet.

Kind.

Beautiful.

Charming.

Outgoing.

Even with our gigantic age difference, I could tell right away that he was nothing like me and that was wonderful.

While I was shy and quiet, he was outgoing and confident.

While I had fears about anything new, he sought it out and embraced it.

I'm not sure how I would've felt about a little brother if I were three when he was born, but at twelve I loved him.

As a shy teenager, I loved how much of my parents' energy he sucked up, energy that would've otherwise been devoted to me.

Plus, I loved how easy it was to make him smile.

Nothing seemed to bother him, and everything made him laugh.

Everyone loved him, and he loved everyone.

And then one day, just a month after his fifth birthday, the fire swept through our home and destroyed our world.

My parents didn't break up because they lost the Burke Ranch.

They didn't break up because they no longer had a retirement plan, or a place to call their own.

Their marriage couldn't survive losing *him*.

We all dealt with the loss in our own ways.

But mostly, we dealt with it by drifting apart.

My parents drifted apart from each other and I drifted apart from them.

I was seventeen and a senior in high school

when it happened, just starting to hear back from colleges about their acceptance decisions.

In addition to the University of Montana, my parents' alma mater and University of Colorado, I had applied to a few schools on the coasts, which my parents were adamantly against.

They wanted me to live in the dorms but be close enough to drive home on weekends.

The flights to the coasts were too expensive and too long.

I was considering giving in and postponing my dream of living in New York City until after graduation.

At the University of Montana, I'd only have to pay state tuition and I got a scholarship, which covered most of that.

So, lack of many student loans was definitely a plus.

Plus, I knew that if I had left when Aspen was so small, then I would miss him way too much and I wanted to be there to see him grow up.

But after the fire, Montana and the West, in general, were no longer an option.

I couldn't be in any place where there was land or mountains or the big blue sky.

It reminded me too much of what I had lost.

Everything reminded me of Aspen.

The only way I could imagine continuing my life after the fire was to move somewhere busy and loud and crowded.

I needed a place that was the exact opposite of Montana and that's what I found in Manhattan.

CHAPTER 8 - HARLEY

THE PRICE OF THINGS...

*a*s much as I love New York, life here isn't very easy.

Basically, it all comes down to money.

I don't have very much of it and everything here is expensive.

Going out to dinner is expensive.

Getting a drink at a bar is expensive.

It's hard to find a cocktail priced under fifteen dollars in this town and I'm not one to let men pay for my drinks.

It's a matter of pride, really.

I don't want to owe anyone a conversation who I am not interested in talking to, so I pay for my own drinks and do what I like.

Unlike Julie, who never passes up an

opportunity for someone else to cover her bills, I always insist on splitting the tab.

You'd think that would be something men found charming, but most of them don't.

Some of them even get offended at the idea.

Still, I do what I think is right, and as a result, I don't go out too much to do anything that costs money.

Especially restaurants.

There's hardly anything worth eating at even a hole in the wall place for under eight dollars a plate, and it costs twelve just to buy a movie ticket to a matinee show.

As a result, I haven't been out for dinner or to the movies in months.

That's what happens when you have to pay the majority of your take-home salary for rent and living expenses and my take-home salary isn't much.

I'm a writer.

I used to call myself an aspiring writer, but not anymore.

Now, I'm the real thing.

I even have a job that pays me to do it.

It's an online job where I write five-hundred word articles about various topics for filler websites.

Like, let's say, a doctor needs some text for his website about whatever it is that he does for a living.

They hire my company to write the copy and then they outsource it to me to actually do it.

The title of my position is content writer and I have written content on topics ranging from window framing to ocean pollution and everything in between.

The pay is fifteen dollars an article, which isn't much given the fact that I usually have to do some research on it first and then compose something readable and error-free.

Many would say it's not really worth the $45,000 a year education I got at Columbia University, but I have grand plans.

I'm not going to be a content writer forever.

I have stories.

I have ideas.

And all of that is going to go into my novel.

Fortunately, I can be a content writer in pajamas and I don't have to get up early or commute anywhere in heels.

Unfortunately, there isn't actually as much work available as I would like there to be and I manage to only clear $2,000 a month.

Not really enough.

"Why don't you just get a job waitressing?" Julie has suggested to me on a number of occasions.

She wants to be a fashion designer, and her unpaid internship at Kate Spade will pave the way.

However, no one in this city really cares that *not* everyone has parents willing to pay for a nice apartment and food while you pursue your dreams with an unpaid internship.

So, Julie works twenty hours a week as a cocktail waitress at one of the hottest clubs in midtown.

It's not like the money she makes there in a week isn't tempting.

Who would say no to $400 to $500 a night on a good weekend for basically smiling, laughing, and serving people drinks?

But I'm not sure if I can do it.

You see, Julie is really outgoing.

And fun.

And gregarious.

And I'm not.

I'm shy and introverted.

Loud music gives me a headache.

Pretending to like people who I don't like gives me a migraine.

So, for now, I compromise and write content.

I don't make as much.

The work isn't exactly easy, but at least I don't have to flutter my eyelashes or wear mini-skirts in the middle of winter.

That is until I have an expected bill that needs to be paid.

Medical insurance has always been a problem mainly due to the cost of buying it every month and then not needing to use it.

$250 a month isn't exactly something I can afford to part with just in case something goes wrong.

Well, then something did.

I had found a big heavy mixer at a flea market that worked like a charm. A month ago, I was trying to move it from the top shelf when disaster struck.

I had a sudden craving for some home baked goods, and though I'm not much of a cook or a baker, I decided to finally get this thing out and give it a go.

Well, the afternoon didn't exactly go as planned.

The mixer was much heavier than I'd thought and I struggled to get it down.

I thought that I was about to drop it when I repositioned my grip.

When I pulled it back up, it threw me off balance and my temple collided with the corner of the cabinet.

Somehow, I managed to climb down to the floor.

My head was throbbing and my vision was a bit blurry, so I stayed down there for a few minutes.

When I felt like it was safe to get up, I pulled myself up by grabbing onto the counter.

I walked to the bathroom to assess the damage.

It can't be more than just a bump.

I'm fine, I told myself.

But when I saw my head in the mirror, I felt queasy.

Blood was running down my face.

Warm, sticky, and dark, it had completely covered my ear and run down my neck.

I don't remember much after that.

What I do remember is Julie kneeling over me and the scared look in her eyes.

She was holding her phone and frantically cursing at being put on hold.

I mumbled something to calm her down.

Then, I realized that I must've passed out.

Finally, after giving up on the prospect of getting an ambulance there, she said that she'd get us a car to take us to the hospital.

She ordered a ride-share on her phone and a driver waited for us downstairs.

I didn't want to go to the hospital because I didn't

have insurance, but she insisted on getting me checked out. Too tired to argue, I went along.

I guess it was a good thing that she made me go because they ended up putting in four stitches to stop the bleeding.

Unfortunately, the whole ordeal also came with a bill of $4,577.35.

CHAPTER 9 - HARLEY

TRYING TO MAKE THINGS WORK...

I do not have an extra forty-six hundred dollars lying around.

Who the hell does?

Receiving that bill was one of the worst days of my life.

How the hell can a simple patch-up job with four stitches cost this much?

I mean, they didn't even do anything.

But it's the emergency room at what I later learned was one of the most expensive hospitals in the city.

Julie took me there because it was the closest one to our apartment.

"You should call them and try to negotiate this down," Julie says. "No one ever pays the full price."

Negotiating a bill?

Is this common knowledge that I'm supposed to negotiate with a hospital about the bill?

This isn't a thrift store or a yard sale.

But what else could I do?

I dread dialing the phone.

First of all, I hate talking on the phone in general, but I hate it even more when it comes to talking to strangers in positions of power over me.

The last time I talked to someone I had talked to a student loan officer about restructuring my student loan and applying for an income-based repayment plan.

But there is no way around it.

I have to lower this bill to something that isn't this if I want to not end up homeless and/or with terrible credit.

The woman on the other end is pleasant enough.

She listens to my sob story and types something into her computer.

Then she comes up with a figure.

"I can get rid of some charges here. And by doing that...the total will come to...$3,478.51. How would you like to pay that?"

I am torn between being grateful for getting a

thousand dollars knocked off my bill and the fact that I still have to come up with the rest.

"I can't pay that amount right now," I mumble.

"Well, I guess we can put you on a payment plan. But it would come with interest. If you pay it over five months, I can set you up with $720 a month."

I'm not ready to do the calculations on the spot and scramble to load the calculator on my phone.

The amount she quotes divided by five months is $695.70, so the rest of that is interest.

But that's beside the point.

If I had an extra $720 a month, I would've bought health insurance in the first place, which would've covered the majority of these charges.

I ask if there are other repayment options, ones with longer times than that?

A year perhaps.

She does some more calculations and offers more numbers.

$356.78 a month over twelve months is the best she can do.

The principal is $289.88 and the rest is interest.

Only she doesn't call it that.

She refers to this amount as fees for creating and servicing the loan.

It's all bullshit and we both know it.

Finally, I agree to it.

What other choice do I have?

She asks for the first amount up front, but I can't give her that.

I tell her to just bill me and she finally agrees.

I guess I should've bought the health insurance in the first place, but the problem is that even if I did, they wouldn't have covered all of these charges.

There would've been a big deductible and I'm not sure that the kind I would've gotten, for three hundred a month, would've covered this emergency room visit. Probably not.

I clench my jaw in anger and try to focus on the article that I need to finish this hour in order to make it worth the $15 that I'm going to be paid for it.

Unfortunately, I can't.

I stare at the blinker for a few minutes, but my mind wanders.

I can't focus.

When I click on the Facebook icon, I know that I'm just going to procrastinate.

No, it's better to just leave the desk and take an actual break.

***

It's cold outside and the wind nips at the tip of my nose.

I don't have a dog, but I like going for walks.

If Julie doesn't have work or somewhere to go, she will stay inside for days and subsist on delivered food.

But I can't do that.

No matter how cold it is out there, no matter how windy, I will put on layers, my coat, a hat, a scarf, and boots and brave the outdoors.

I don't know what it is about being outside, but it always rejuvenates me.

I've had my online job for close to ten months now and at first it was tempting to just huddle up and never get out of my pajamas day after day.

You'd be surprised how easy it is to never go outside if you live in a city like New York.

Back home, there are only a few restaurants that deliver and it's really up to you to run your own errands.

But in Manhattan, you can pretty much hire anyone to do anything for you, allowing you the time to veg out on the couch.

When I started this job, I decided to forgo my walks and instead work more.

But I quickly noticed that my productivity went down considerably if I just stayed inside.

There's something about the process of getting dressed, braving the elements, and taking yourself on a two mile walk around the park that really perks me up and allows me to crank out the articles even faster afterward.

WHEN TWILIGHT COMES...

So, here I am again.

Darkness is falling.

It just rained.

The air is full of moisture and I'm making my way toward Riverside Park, which is about a five-minute walk from my place on 105th Street.

I live on the Upper West Side, not far away from where I used to live when I attended Columbia.

I know that Brooklyn is the popular, hip place to be, but I like it here.

Julie prefers downtown where there's more happening, and she probably wouldn't live with me if we hadn't found such a cheap place.

Riverside Park is my favorite park in New York.

I probably prefer it even over Central Park

because it's smaller and more manageable to navigate.

It runs all along the Hudson River for about four miles.

Some ambitious runners like to make the loop from top to bottom, but I usually just go a mile or two.

What's great about Manhattan is that in this sea of people, there are a lot of parks which are actually big enough to lose yourself.

And luckily for me, very few people, besides runners and dog owners, venture out into the cold on unforgiving late February days.

The gray, listless Hudson River runs to my right and small enclosures where dog owners can let their dogs run free with other dogs of similar size run along my left.

There are only a few dogs here now and even fewer runners.

Even though I'm wearing a thick scarf and the top of my coat is cinched up tightly, the wind still manages to get in and chill me down to my bones.

But I continue to walk.

I have made a decision.

I am not going back home until I figure out some way to pay for this medical bill.

* * *

THE PROCESS of figuring out what to do could've probably taken less time with an internet connection, but the brisk walk definitely clears my head.

Yes, the bill is high.

Yes, I have no way to pay it.

But that doesn't mean I don't have options.

The only option I don't have is to mope.

I also can't tell my parents what's going on because they have their own problems.

Besides, in their mind there's only one solution; to move back home.

It's pretty much the only thing they agree on nowadays and that is one of the many reasons why I can't.

There's another option though.

I could take Julie up on that position she offered me.

The cocktail waitressing job with the big tips.

I don't really want to dress up and do that night after night, but it might be my only choice.

Besides, it will get me out of my sweats and out of the house, as Julie says.

Maybe then I will even meet a guy.

57

I can hear her words in my head and I can't help but roll my eyes at the imaginary vision of her.

Guys, or rather men, are a big deal for Julie.

I guess they are for me as well, but it's different.

I just have my own issues with dating.

The thing is that men our age seem to only be interested in one thing in this town - a hookup.

And Julie loves that.

I would be shocked if she ever went on more than two dates with the same guy, let alone said that she was 'dating' someone.

But me?

I'm a bit different.

Old-fashioned, I guess.

I'm not looking for a husband.

There's no way I'm ready for anything like that.

But it would be nice to actually meet someone and spend a significant amount of time with him.

Especially, if I liked him and he liked me back.

When I get back home, Julie is in the kitchen heating up some leftovers in the microwave.

It smells good and I think I'll have the same for dinner as well.

Neither of us are much for cooking and with the plethora of good quality convenience food that New York has to offer, we don't really have to be.

"Logan asked me to move in with him!" Julie shrieks at the top of her lungs.

Logan?

Who's Logan?

Suddenly, I remember.

"Didn't you just meet like two weeks ago?"

"Three. But we've been spending practically all of our time together."

That I didn't really know.

Besides the fact that we get along really well, another great perk of having Julie as a roommate is that she often goes back to Staten Island for a night or two to visit her family, and recently she has been spending a lot of time at Logan's place.

Those days away give us space and makes sharing one room not feel so crowded.

"He asked me to move in with him!" Julie says.

Her voice is high and loud and, for a second, I'm not sure if she is actually excited about the question or appalled.

Neither would surprise me.

A big wide smile forms on her face and I know the answer.

"I love him," Julie says. "I really do!"

I nod, rattling my brain for something to say in return.

But nothing comes to mind.

Instead, I just stare into space.

"Harley? Aren't you going to say something, Harley?"

I force myself to snap out of it and give her a reassuring smile.

"I'm really happy for you. Really."

Oblivious to my real reaction, she zaps a cup of tea in the microwave and takes a bite off her plate.

Then she starts to tell me all about their plans.

Logan works for an investment bank and he lives in a fifteen-hundred square foot apartment on the Lower East Side.

It's a two-bedroom so there will be a guest room, and a place for me to "crash anytime I want." Her words, not mine.

Crossing Central Park for a visit doesn't seem like much of an imposition to me, but you'd be surprised how many New Yorkers do not feel this way.

One of the main reasons why Julie resisted going out with Logan in the first place was that he lived across the park.

CHAPTER 11 - HARLEY

COMPLICATIONS...

*A*s Julie talks about the spaciousness of his apartment and how he can afford the place all on his own so she won't have to contribute to much except food and utilities, I can't help but feel like I'm being tossed aside.

What about me?

I'm not upset just because she's moving out with her boyfriend, even though I will miss her.

I'm mainly upset because this move will turn my life upside down.

I can barely afford my share of our apartment as it is, and if she moves out, then I'll be forced to either look for a cheaper place or find someone who is interested in sharing a studio with a total stranger.

"What about our lease?" I ask. "You know I can't afford this place on my own."

The thought of how this will impact me has apparently never occurred to her until this very moment.

"Oh, shit," she says, deflated.

Julie is kind, but she can also be a bit obtuse and self-centered.

If I want her to understand my position then I need to explain.

"The thing is that I just found out that I'm going to have to pay the hospital like thirty-five hundred dollars for that whole debacle, which comes out to about three-hundred and sixty dollars a month extra over twelve months. I didn't even know how I was going to cover that in addition to paying my share of the rent. But if you move out..."

I let my words trail off.

I don't know how to continue because I don't know what would happen if she moved out.

There is no way I could afford this place.

And finding a person who is willing to move into a studio with a perfect stranger is a tall order even in this city.

Julie listens and nods her head.

But I can tell that she doesn't have much of an answer either.

"I'm sorry, but it's going to be okay, Harley. It will work out...somehow."

I take a deep breath.

Now, I feel like a bit of a fool.

She is sharing something fun and exciting about her life and I'm making it all about me.

She doesn't call me on it, but I feel bad, nevertheless.

Suddenly, it feels like a cereal for dinner type of night.

I fight my battles with processed foods and enriched-flour carbohydrates as much as the next girl, but I can handle only one battle at a time.

I grab a box with granola clusters and dried cranberries and don't even bother with a bowl.

I dig my hand right in and curl up with it on the couch.

"What can I do?" Julie asks. "Is there anything I can do?"

"Stay?" I ask. She gives me a forced smile.

"I'm going to miss you, Julie. I mean that."

We have been roommates since our sophomore year of college and then again our senior year after she came back from a semester abroad.

63

After graduation, we decided to get a place together.

That apartment turned into another and another, and while the places changed, the roommates stayed the same.

It's an unusual thing to like the person you live with more than your apartment.

I can still remember when we first saw this place in September.

Neither of us were looking for a new place, but it was in a more convenient neighborhood, close to both parks and not too far for her to commute.

$1800 was a bit much to pay for a studio, but it's a large studio, almost four hundred square feet.

We shared a small dorm room in college so the fact that it was one big room didn't really phase either of us.

Julie gives me a little hug and tells me that she will miss me, too.

"Okay, I've had enough of my moping for one night. Tell me more about Logan and his great place."

* * *

THE FOLLOWING MORNING, I start looking for work.

I can't get anymore work writing content articles with the company that I'm with, so I search for others online.

I open an account on three of those online work sites where freelancers can find work.

In one, I offer my services of composing, writing, and editing resumes and cover letters.

Ironic, isn't it?

In another, I offer to edit high school and college papers.

Research papers.

College application essays.

English papers.

Once I start my profiles, I immediately have a few inquiries and by the end of the day, I book a few jobs.

Three resume editing jobs at five dollars each.

Two cover letter composing jobs at fifteen dollars each.

Not bad.

I complete all the work that evening in addition to my usual content writing and finally close my computer at ten p.m., completely exhausted.

Perhaps, I shouldn't have worked so hard today given that I have to go and try out working with Julie tonight.

But sometimes, I just lose myself in the process of doing one thing after another and time gets away from me.

My hands are throbbing from banging on the keyboard and from running my index finger on the mousepad and I elevate them above my head.

That's what you do for swelling, right?

Does it work for the beginning of carpal tunnel as well?

"What are you doing?" Julie bursts in the front door, looking frantic. "You're not even ready."

I look at the clock.

"We still have an hour."

"And we're going to need every minute of that to get you ready."

I roll my eyes.

Am I really such a lost cause?

CHAPTER 12 - HARLEY

MORE COMPLICATIONS...

Much to no one's surprise, I am not an amazing waitress.

I am clumsy and not a particularly great multitasker.

I can't simultaneously flirt, take an order, and upsell an expensive bottle of vodka.

The place is so loud I can barely hear what people order.

Handling drinks with condensation on them, my hands are always wet, which makes my notepad wet, making my pen practically unusable.

And remembering what seven people around the same table want with their particular details about how much ice to include, and what kind, and whether or not they want a lemon is practically impossible.

"I'm so bad at this!" I scream into Julie's ear when she waltzes over, making the job look easy and flawless.

"It's your first day; you'll get the hang of it."

I shake my head.

I'm not so sure, but I get back to it.

My customers aren't happy with my service but as the night drags on luckily, they are getting too drunk to notice the specifics.

Around two-thirty in the morning, when my feet are throbbing almost as much as my head, someone bumps into me as I am carrying a serving tray with five drinks.

They all go barreling down to the floor and a girl who isn't too steady on her feet slips and lands right on the glass.

The rest of the evening is a blur.

Julie and our co-workers help me clean up and reassure me that everything is okay and that this happens to the best of them.

The only problem is that Julie has been working here since college off and on and hasn't dropped one tray, let alone severely injured a patron.

The manager comes over and lets me know that I can clock out for today.

My trial period is over for now and I doubt that I'm going to have another chance.

I wasn't cut out for this job, even before I sent a girl to the emergency room.

Julie doesn't get off until four, so I call a ride-share to come pick me up.

It will cost $15 to get home.

Perfect.

I'm not sure how much a cab would cost, but what I like about ride-shares is that I get to see the picture and the name of the driver before I get in and exactly how much the price will be.

It's also nice to be able to get it through an app on my phone and pay through the app, including tips, rather than hailing a cab and scrounging around for cash, which I never have.

A black Honda arrives a few minutes later.

It matches the car on my phone.

After nodding hello, I sit back in the back and zone out.

I've had a really long day and it takes great energy to summon the strength to even keep my eyes open.

"Late night, huh?" the driver asks.

"Mmm-mmm."

I really don't want to make small talk.

Please, just leave me alone to my thoughts.

Most drivers are pretty good about doing that, but this one doesn't get the message.

"That's unusual for you."

His words catch me off guard.

My whole body tenses up.

Suddenly, his voice doesn't just sound vaguely familiar, I recognize it immediately.

It's *him*.

When I look in the rearview mirror, my worst fears are confirmed.

I reach for the door handle, but he presses the lock button.

"What are you doing here?"

"Just working, you know? Trying to make a living."

"Under a false identity?"

"Well, you wouldn't have ever gotten into my car if you knew who I was, right?" He laughs.

His voice and laugh are just as grating as ever. But he has lost some weight.

"What do you want?" I demand to know in the sternest tone possible.

My heart is beating a million miles per minute,

but I can't let him see that.

I can't act scared.

I have to be strong.

And I also need to come up with a plan.

The windows of the car are conveniently tinted.

The door of the back seat is locked.

"I miss you," he says. "Don't you miss me?"

I haven't seen him for awhile.

I actually thought that he had found another hobby besides following me.

Stalking me.

But apparently he was just trying to come up with a better plan.

"No, I can't say I have."

"Oh, c'mon. I know that's not true. Don't tell me you haven't thought about me at all in all this time?"

"Fuck you."

"You shouldn't use that kind of language, young lady."

My blood runs cold.

He's different.

More confident.

Arrogant.

"You must've been following me for a very long time to put this plan into action."

"I'm glad you noticed, it did take a bit. I can't tell

71

you how many times you didn't choose my car to give you a ride. I was losing hope actually."

I am drenched in sweat and my legs are sticking to the leather seats.

I clench my fists.

"Where are you taking me?"

"Somewhere special," he says. "Somewhere we can be alone. You'll see. It's a surprise."

I have to get out of this car.

I can't let him take me there.

If I don't...I may not be able to escape.

As he speeds down the empty streets following one green light after another, I feel my chances diminishing.

No one knows where I am and no one will know that I'm missing until Julie comes home.

And that won't be for hours.

Suddenly, a red light catches him off guard.

He presses on the brakes at the last moment, stopping so suddenly the car screeches to a halt.

He hits the unlock button by accident and I see my chance.

I open the door and make a run for it.

My workday proceeds as any other. There's a conference call with my Chief Financial Officer talking about the quarterly revenue projections and expected profits.

He mentions that we have yet another offer to take the company public, which I have no interest in doing.

He presses me a bit, but then lets go.

The problem with taking the company public, from my point of view, is that I will suddenly have to answer to stakeholders.

Today, I am the biggest investor in the company and I'm the only who I have to answer to.

In fact, I grew this company in such a way that I

didn't actually acquire any additional investment capital.

I was able to do this because I lived on a tiny salary and invested any profits I had back into growing the company.

Though going public would make me an even richer man and would give me millions, if not billions, of actual cash and a very lucrative salary as CEO, it would also involve other people, hordes of other people, in my decision-making.

Throughout the day, I answer emails, read spreadsheets, and make and approve other acquisition decisions.

There are a number of online magazines that we own that are not doing that well and my team and I discuss what we should do about that.

Most argue that the best thing to do is let them go, but I believe that we just didn't give them the right support.

Perhaps it would be best to fold that magazine under the umbrella of another one that's a lot more popular.

All the meetings are done by five that evening, but my workday continues.

I take a little break and order some delivery from

my favorite Indian restaurant, and then return to my laptop.

I'm the first one to admit that I am a workaholic, but I am not someone who will apologize for it.

There was a time when I used to feel guilty about all the time that I spent working.

I felt torn between my passion and my family.

But that's no more.

I don't have a family anymore; I just have my work.

Around ten, I close my laptop and stretch out my arms around my head.

My back has cramped up from being in a sitting position all day and I missed my workout downstairs.

I'll make it up tomorrow, I promise myself.

In the kitchen, I grab the rest of the paneer pakora and flip on the television.

There isn't much on, so I put on Netflix to watch something without commercials.

Suddenly, the doorbell goes off.

I am not expecting anyone and everyone I order from knows that I don't want any direct contact.

But the bell goes off again.

And again.

And again.

I walk over to the massive double doors and look through the peephole.

A woman is standing on my stoop, shivering in the rain.

She is dressed in a mini-skirt and a tank top.

Her arms are covered in goose bumps and her hair is drenched.

Her teeth are practically chattering with each move.

She keeps looking behind her, and then suddenly her movements get more frantic.

Instead of ringing the doorbell, she starts knocking on the door.

"Please! Somebody help me! Please! You have to open the door!" she pleads.

Her pleading voice invokes a sense of irritation within me.

Why is she here?

What is she doing bothering me?

Doesn't she know that I don't see people?

"Go away!" I bark. "No one is home."

As soon as she hears me answer, her voice gets even louder and higher.

"Please, sir, please, you have to let me in. I can't go back there. He's after me."

I hesitate for a moment.

I've never had anyone come to my door like this.

In fact, in the four years that I've lived alone, I haven't had anyone come to the door at all and refuse to leave.

"Call the police."

"I can't."

"I can call the police for you."

"Yes, please do. But first, you have to help me. They won't come in time."

I look out of the peephole to try to see what, if anything, is around her.

I see something move.

And somewhere in the distance, I see the rustling of bushes and a lone figure.

"Go away!" the woman screams. "Get away from me!"

But the figure doesn't leave.

He approaches and grabs her by her hair.

He pulls her down the stairs and toward the sidewalk.

No, no, no.

I shake my head.

I swing the door open and run him down.

I punch him once in the face and once in the gut.

The woman yells as he pulls her down to the pavement with him by her hair.

I unclasp his grip. She lets out a loud sigh.

"Are you okay?"

She nods, still stunned from what happened.

The guy tries to run, but I put out my leg and trip him.

He falls face first onto the pavement and blood starts to gush out of his nose and onto the pavement.

"I'm sorry I didn't believe you." I sit down on top of him to keep him from fleeing.

Then I pull out my phone and dial 911.

CHAPTER 14 - JACKSON

WHEN THEY COME...

While we wait for the cops to arrive, the woman doesn't speak and I don't ask her any questions.

The sooner that this whole ordeal is over the better.

I haven't spoken to another person in real life in years and suddenly I feel a pang of anxiety building somewhere in the back of my throat.

I'm angry at her for forcing me out here.

I'm angry at him for attacking her.

Quickly, but surely, claustrophobia is setting in.

It's as if being outside of my front door is making my whole world feel like it's about to cave in.

I look back at my house.

The stoop is freshly swept and cleaned, and the bushes are pruned.

My home is calling back to me and I feel its pull as if it were a magnet.

But as soon as I let my body off the man even a little bit, he stirs.

I know that if I make a move to escape this place, he will take off, probably never to be heard from again.

The cops finally arrive.

They tell me to let him go, but I'm not sure if they are prepared to catch him if he takes off.

I hesitate, so they tell me to let go of him more sternly.

This time, I comply.

Why am I getting so involved?

My job is done.

All I have to do is answer their questions and then go back inside.

When one of the police officers takes the guy into the back of his car, the detective who arrives a little bit later to the scene pulls me aside to ask me some questions.

I tell her exactly what happened.

Nothing more, nothing less.

I don't know why that man was after this woman.

I don't know why she ran up to my stoop.

And frankly, I don't care.

"You seem a little agitated, sir," the detective says in an accusatory manner.

"I just want to go home."

"Is this an imposition, sir?"

This makes me mad.

"A woman ringing my doorbell and insisting that I answer it because some maniac is attacking her? And when I do, I pull her away from him and then have to pin him down and wait for you all to arrive at the scene. Yes, I would say that this whole thing is a fucking imposition."

I decide not to go further into the details of my life.

I don't tell her that my throat is so dry it's about to close up.

I don't tell her that my hands are clammy, not from the chill that's in the air, but by the virtue of the fact that I'm here talking to what feels like ten people at once and I haven't spoken to anyone like this in years.

To tell her any of this would just disclose my anxiety further.

No, I have to pretend like everything is okay so they can let me go.

For a moment, I debate whether I should invite any of them inside.

Perhaps, I'd feel better being there, in my safe place, but finally I decide against it.

I don't want more attention.

I don't want to have to kick them out.

I don't want their dirty boots and dirty questions in my castle of solitude.

No, they are not welcome there.

If they want to ask me more questions, they can ask them out here.

As we continue to talk and I continue to repeat my story over and over again, my eyes drift to the back of the ambulance where the woman is sitting.

Someone has given her a gray wool blanket to warm her up. Wrapped up in it, she looks even more soggy and innocent.

When she hangs her head, her long, dark, knotted hair separates in thick strands and falls in her face.

She pushes it out of the way, but she doesn't pull it up in a bun, so it quickly comes back.

I wait for her to lift her head, and when she does, I see her hazel eyes.

Still moist from an onslaught of tears, they shine brightly.

She focuses her gaze on me and mouths the words, 'thank you'.

I give her a slight nod in return.

Finally, the detective runs out of questions and lets me go, handing me a card in case I remember anything else.

I take it and walk up the stairs to my front door.

Though the commotion outside has brought out a number of my neighbors, I have no interest in spending more time out here than I absolutely have to.

Back in my sanctuary, I head straight to my liquor cabinet and pour myself a glass of whiskey.

I look at the way the dark golden-brown liquid slushes over the ice and then inhale it.

It runs down my throat and, for a moment, takes away all the pain that talking to those people has brought back.

After I finish the glass, I take a deep breath and close my eyes.

A loud thump on the door destroys my moment of serenity.

"Go away!" I yell loud enough for them to hear. "I already answered all of your questions."

But the knock continues.

When I don't answer it, they press the doorbell.

"Go away!"

"I'm really sorry to bother you," a familiar voice says from the other side.

It belongs to the woman whom I helped.

If you hate to bother me then don't, I am tempted to reply.

But her pleading stirs something inside of me.

If I had helped her when she first showed up, she wouldn't have been attacked by that man.

A pang of guilt rushes through me.

I crack the door.

"I just want to thank you. For everything that you have done. I'm sorry for showing up on your stoop like this and for bringing you into this whole mess."

Why was that guy after you? I want to ask.

But I bite my tongue.

That would just prolong the conversation and I can't have that.

"It's okay. You're welcome," I say and go to close the door.

But the woman wedges her foot inside to stop it.

"I mean it. Really. You saved my life."

She looks at me with her piercing hazel eyes.

They are almond-shaped and a little bit tilted at the ends, and absolutely mesmerizing.

I have the feeling that if I let myself go, I could lose myself in them forever.

"I understand. I have to go now."

I push her foot out and close the door.

CHAPTER 15 - JACKSON

WHEN I'M ALONE AGAIN...

It's strange being alone again after that.

I spent years orchestrating my life so that I would never see another person and then one day it all crashes down around me.

One day, a knock on my door changes everything.

And yet, changes nothing.

It has been two days since the incident and my life has returned to normal,

My hours are filled with work and whatever time I have left over is devoted to lifting weights in my gym and unwinding with a little bit of television.

I have my old life back, except that I don't.

My thoughts are occupied, no hijacked, by *her*.

That woman who appeared on my front door one day asking for help.

That woman I should've helped earlier.

That woman who I shouldn't have closed the door on after.

How can I explain to her that I wasn't just being an asshole?

How can I explain that I felt like if I stood there talking to her for a moment longer, my heart would jump out of my chest?

The walls were closing in all around me and if I saw one more flashing light and heard one more voice, then the little gulps of breath that I did manage to inhale would disappear completely.

At that moment, I couldn't explain any of those things.

I just needed to get her to stop talking and to go away.

I've had moments like this before, of course, right after *it* happened.

There were instances that made me feel like this and the only way to make them go away was to retreat into my private space.

The difference between then and now is that no matter how rude I was to those people my thoughts didn't linger on them afterward.

Yet, my mind keeps drifting back to *her*.

* * *

ANOTHER DAY PASSES, and I find myself incapable of focusing on work.

In the afternoon, I tell Phillips that I'm taking the rest of the day off and head down to the gym.

After an hour of bench presses, leg lifts, and calf exercises, I feel drained.

But it's a good kind of tired that comes from sheer physical exhaustion rather than boredom.

I take the elevator back upstairs and collapse into a recliner with a bottle of water and a tablet.

But as soon as I turn it on, my thoughts immediately return to the woman.

Her soggy hair.

Her limp body.

Her bright eyes.

Her attempts to thank me and my rude reaction in the face of nothing but kindness.

And then something else comes to mind.

I don't even know her name.

I *have* to find out her name.

Things like this don't just happen in this part of town without something appearing about it online.

I Google my house and the word 'attack'.

And there it is.

A Minetta Media owned magazine has an article about the incident.

There's a quote from the detective, the mention of my name, and even a quote from the victim.

Usually, victims have the right to remain anonymous, but this woman doesn't.

Her name is Harley Burke.

The only thing I really want to say about this whole thing is how grateful I am to Mr. Jackson Ludlow for helping me. He really saved my life.

That's the quote that the writer attributes to her.

No one asked me for a quote in return, probably because they doubted that I would give one.

I read her words over and over again and they bathe me in unfamiliar warmth.

Reclusive Billionaire saves woman from attack.

That's the headline, and not something that I am particularly fond of.

If it were anyone else then I would be angry that they would dare bring me into the public eye.

Yet, at this moment, all I can think about is that her name is Harley Burke and she lives on the Upper West Side.

What is it about her? I wonder.

What is it about her that makes me want to find her and apologize?

I wouldn't feel this way toward anyone else.

I know.

I've been rude to a lot of people.

And yet, with her, everything is different.

I look her up online and find a number of articles attributed to her.

So, she's a writer?

Her articles cover a variety of topics, pretty typical for content writing mills that pay their writers shit and make big bucks on useless websites that provide very little value to readers.

Their only real value is to the owners as click bait sites with cheap clicks.

I try to find a blog or some videos on YouTube and other sites, but nothing comes up.

Then I look her up on social media.

She doesn't have a very carefully curated social media account, and that makes it so much more realistic and organic.

There are pictures of her at birthday parties and dinners with friends, walking in the park, visiting Philadelphia.

There are pictures of her laughing and smiling,

and some are the serious, artsy ones with pursed lips and serious expressions.

The more I look, the more I want to know more.

Who is she really?

What does she like to do?

What makes her laugh?

CHAPTER 16 - JACKSON

WHEN I HAVE TO FIND HER...

Harley Burke continues to pollute my thoughts for the next few days, no matter how hard I try to push her out.

I have no business devoting my time to her.

She doesn't matter.

There isn't anything special about her, so why the hell can't I stop thinking about her?

I don't know the answer to this question.

All I know is that I need to see her again.

Briefly, I consider the possibility of leaving my home and going to find her.

But I quickly reconsider.

That's not an option.

I don't need to make this anymore complicated than it has to be.

TANGLED UP IN ICE

I will just ask her to come see me, that is if I can find her number online.

I start the search, and then close my laptop.

After I was so rude to her that night, I doubt that she will be particularly open to taking time from her day to come here.

I wouldn't.

No, I need a better plan.

I run through different ideas in my mind until I stumble onto a good one.

She's looking for writing jobs.

What if I create a dummy job application for a job that I know she'll want and she will be the only one who I will consider?

Now, what kind of job would Harley Burke apply for?

It could be a position for a content writer, but that would be a safe bet.

No, I need something she can't stop thinking about.

I could go with more of a journalism position, but I'm not sure if that's something that she has the qualifications for.

No, I need something better.

I go to the kitchen to make myself a cup of coffee.

And then, right when I stand in front of the open

refrigerator, it hits me.

Of course.

Research position.

Nothing too fancy, doable by almost anyone with a bachelor's degree, and yet with astronomical pay.

I have to make her want this more than anything in the world.

What would a real salary pay for this?

Definitely not $15 per hour.

I mean, who the hell can live on that in New York City anyway?

And then suddenly, I remember that I lived on a lot less when I first moved here.

"Don't be such an asshole, Jackson," I mutter out loud.

I open my phone and find some of the recent postings that my human resources department has put out.

Most don't mention the pay, but I have to.

Finally, I settle on $50 per hour and mention that the job pays that well because it requires discretion.

Discretion is a metaphorical term used in job applications to convey that the job requires secrecy, usually implying that you will work for a high-profile person.

I guess that part of it is true.

. . .

***

Days pass without much of a result.

Either I did not post the posting on the right sites or she's not looking for a position anymore.

Of course, there's another possibility: Harley saw the post and decided to pass because she has other options.

I decide to give it a week before moving on to plan B, whatever the hell that will be.

What I do get instead of Harley is about a thousand emails from other interested parties.

Most are from New York, but some are from elsewhere.

Almost all are aspiring writers looking to make it big in the city of dreams.

I feel bad for wasting their time, but only for a moment.

I continue to search their messages for signs of Harley.

All to no avail.

And then...just as I am about to give up hope, I get an email.

An actual email from Harley stating her credentials, experience, and interest in the position.

Even though I want to write her back immediately, I need to maintain this charade so I force myself to wait a few hours before getting back to her.

The email I compose is short, sweet, and right to the point.

WHEN CAN *you come in for an interview?*

TO WHICH SHE RESPONDS, *anytime.*

HOW ABOUT THIS *afternoon at four?*

PERFECT. *Where?*

SHIT.

This, I did not anticipate.

If I give her my address, she'll know that it's the place where she got attacked.

If I ask to meet her somewhere else then...I'd have to *be* somewhere else.

CHAPTER 17 - HARLEY

WHEN TIME DOESN'T HEAL...

*T*ime is supposed to heal all wounds, but it seems to have only healed the physical ones.

For a long time, my mind runs in circles as if it's in a loop.

I'm at the club.

I'm working.

I'm messing up.

I'm uncomfortable and cold in my short skirt and sleeveless arms.

The music is too loud, and I can barely hear myself think, let alone hear what the guests are ordering.

I ask them for their orders a few times and I have trouble writing them down in my notepad.

Why are these details important?

And why do I keep coming back to them?

They're not really.

But I can't take myself to the rest of the night.

The memories come in flashes.

The car.

The guy.

The inappropriate jokes, which make my skin crawl.

At first, I think he's just a creep, the type of guy who likes to make women uncomfortable.

The type of guy who if you confront him about what he's saying will just say, oh, I'm just joking.

What's the matter, you can't take a joke?

But then something changes.

His voice takes a different tone.

And that's when the memories really form a flood.

They come all at once and way too fast.

Like a waterfall that I can't fight.

All I can do instead is swim away from it.

I try to bury myself in work, but it's all to no avail.

There's no point.

So I put on the television and tune out.

When I get tired of watching show after show, I turn up the music.

Loud.

I have to fill the whole apartment with something in order to drown out my thoughts.

* * *

MORE TIME PASSES, yet my thoughts do not dissipate.

They continue to haunt me.

There are glimpses of light, however.

Instead of the man who attacked me, I focus on the man who saved me.

He should've opened the door earlier.

He should've listened to my pleas in the beginning.

But he refused.

Yet, I am grateful that he did come to my rescue when he finally did.

What would've happened otherwise?

And again, darkness descends.

My thoughts keep returning to him.

Does he have a family?

Does he live in that mansion all by himself?

Isn't he a bit too young to own a house that extravagant?

I found out his name from the detectives.

Jackson Ludlow.

Apparently, he owns a big media company and is a multi-millionaire. Really rich.

In any case, he probably has more money than he knows what to do with.

It would be a lie to say that I'm not a bit jealous.

Not of his mansion, or his closet, or anything like that.

I don't really care about money in that way.

What I'm jealous about is just his freedom to not worry about paying for his necessities.

It's not like I want to buy some $400 boots.

No, I just don't want to struggle to make rent on a studio apartment and for my medical bills.

Whatever problems he has, paying for basic necessities is definitely not one of them.

And of that, I'm jealous.

"How are you feeling today?" Julie comes in for the last bit of her stuff.

She wasn't planning to move out so soon, but I guess being around my mopey self wasn't something that was particularly appealing to her.

She had an excuse, of course.

Logan is going away for work and she needs to stay there for two weeks to babysit his cat.

She thought about just packing a bag, but then decided to just move in.

What's the point of moving in the week
after that?

Her reasoning is sound, of course, and she will
be paying me rent for a few months in advance here,
but I still want her to stay.

I want someone to be with me, to distract me
from all this shit that my life has recently
become.

"I'm feeling okay."

She walks around the living room and collects
my dirty plates and other garbage that I produced
over the last few days.

"I'm not sure you are."

I shrug. "Want to stay longer and hang out? You
can bring the cat here."

She shakes her head. "You know I can't. The
landlord will flip out."

"I wish he didn't live right next door," I say.

"Okay, how about this, if you're still feeling shitty
in two weeks then I'll move back in. But if I do that
then you have to do everything I say."

I think about that for a moment.

That doesn't sound like a terrible plan.

But wait, what does she mean I have to do
everything she says?

"Putting on something besides pajamas. Taking a

shower. Putting on makeup. Going outside once in a while," Julie explains.

The first couple of suggestions sound difficult enough, but the last one?

No.

Not for a long time.

"You don't have to go out after dark, but you do have go outside. You can't become one of those shut-ins they feature on reality shows."

I shrug.

Why would that be so bad?

"Okay, I have to go. Logan is taking off soon," Julie says, grabbing the last of her stuff.

It's a laundry basket filled with knickknacks that didn't fit well into any other boxes that she shuttled over to the Lower East Side in the previous days.

I nod and flip the television back on.

"Promise me that you will do some writing today."

"Why do you care about that?" I ask, taken a little aback by her request.

"It doesn't have to be for work. Just write anything. I know how much writing makes you feel better."

"Okay, bye," I say with a shrug.

"And promise me that you will go outside sometime."

Julie pushes a bit too far.

"Um, yeah, right," I say sarcastically.

"Okay, promise me you'll take a shower!"

"Bye, Mom!" I yell as she closes the front door.

CHAPTER 18 - HARLEY

WHEN DOING SOMETHING HELPS...

I turn up one of the recorded episodes of a reality show that I've been watching for a few days, but my mind is on something else.

For once, it's not on what happened, but on something else entirely. Writing.

Julie is right.

Writing is something I've always done to make myself feel better.

Ever since I was a little girl, I filled journals upon journals with thoughts, ideas, poems, and stories.

Some of my journals are on the computer, but most are written by hand.

I go to my desk and pick out a new journal for the occasion.

I have a number of brand new ones waiting

and this time I opt for a vegan leather one with a fake suede strap that you can use to tie it up on the side.

Since journals are the only thing I ever really indulge in as far as extravagant purchases go, I try to be mindful of my decisions.

I try to limit my use of animal products so a few months ago I made the decision to stop buying leather journals and instead opting for fabric, cloth, paper, or vegan leather.

When I pick it up, I remember everything about the moment that I got it.

It was from a little boutique that specializes in paper arts and when I bought it, the saleswoman wrapped it in brown Kraft paper and twine.

I remember the first time I touched it and how much I had to have it even though I couldn't justify spending $45 on it.

And I remember how it felt to put away $5 each week from my food budget so that I could afford to get it as a birthday present to myself at the end of the month.

Yes, this feels right.

This is the journal that I'm going to write in today.

I carefully open the distressed vegan leather flap

and run my fingers over the ruggedness of the hand torn pages.

I flip the first page, in case I need to mark it with a date and title later on and press my pen to the top.

The words quickly start to pile out of me.

I describe the mansion bordering on Central Park.

I describe the lonely man living inside of it.

The recluse.

For a moment, I wonder.

Are you lonely or are you just alone?

People confuse these things, but they are very different from one another.

It is only after the attack that I really started to feel lonely by myself.

But before that?

Being alone had its benefits.

In fact, I loved it.

Those weekends that Julie went to Staten Island.

I lived for those.

I had the place to myself.

A place to be alone.

A place to read, write, and think.

Is that why you are a recluse, I wonder.

Is that why you do not leave this mansion?

I've heard rumors about Jackson Ludlow, but I

have no idea if he is anything like this man I'm describing.

And frankly, I don't really care.

What matters instead is that this man who I am writing about on these tea-stained pages is real.

Ten minutes quickly become thirty and then an hour.

The words are spilling out of me so fast that I can barely keep up.

My hand cramps up, but I shake it out and continue turning the pages.

My handwriting becomes blurry and difficult to read, but the thoughts stay with me.

Most of them are not so much sentences, but a collection of ideas of this man and his life.

When I get another cramp, I stop for a moment to stretch my fingers and crack my knuckles.

Then something occurs to me.

Where is this story going?

Nowhere in particular.

Actually, it's not really a story at all.

Just thoughts about this man I invented.

But is it a real invention? I mean, I did meet him.

Jackson Ludlow.

All I do know is that he is this illusive man with a lot of wealth who is somewhat of a recluse.

At least, that's what the one article I could find on him mentioned.

Is he really a recluse?

And why?

Suddenly, I am walking a tight rope between fiction and reality.

The thing that I noticed about the process of writing a long time ago, and what really appeals to me about it, is how it crystallizes my thoughts about whatever it is that I'm thinking about.

You'd think that given how we had met, I would not want to see Jackson again.

But the opposite is actually true.

My thoughts keep returning to him.

And with each return, I remember more and more.

I remember how twisted his lips got in a look of shock when he saw that man pull me back by my hair.

I remember the rage that I saw in his eyes when he attacked him in return.

I remember how soft yet strong his hands felt when he helped me back to my feet.

I remember how his dark curls bounced with each move.

And then there's something else.

But this memory dances around, remaining just out of reach.

I search my mind, trying to catch it, but I can't.

It's like that feeling when you know you're forgetting something important but you still can't remember what it is.

I pick up my pen and let words flow out of me without much thought or reason.

WHEN HE GOT UP, *his shirt blew open slightly by the wind and that's when I saw it.*

Just below his collarbones.

The scars rose up and down with each breath as his strong muscles pressed against his shirt.

But then another gust of wind came through and he buttoned his shirt, hiding his secrets beneath it.

THESE WORDS ARE NO LONGER about my fictional character.

They are about Jackson Ludlow.

This is exactly as it had happened.

I had forgotten about this until this very moment, but as soon as I lift the pen off the paper, all I can focus on are those scars above his collarbone.

Where did he get them?

Why are they there?

Who hurt him?

CHAPTER 19 - HARLEY

WHEN I APPLY FOR A JOB...

Night falls but I continue to write and think.

My fictional character has suddenly morphed into someone very much unlike the man I started out with.

I look up Jackson Ludlow online and incorporate as much as I can about him into my journal.

I don't know why I have this desire to learn more about him, but something is pushing me toward it.

I *want* to know more.

And when I learn more, I realize that I *need* to know even more.

Finally, after close to three hours, I decide to take a break.

I can barely lift my right hand up, let alone unfurl my fingers.

Perhaps I overdid it somewhat, I joke to myself.

When I head to the kitchen to make a snack, I realize that darkness has set in.

I stare out of the window in amazement.

Usually, as soon as twilight starts to fall, I go around and pull down the blinds and close the curtains.

Then I turn on all the lights to make it as bright as possible inside.

I've been doing this religiously everyday since the incident to make myself a little more comfortable being alone at home. Everyday except today.

Tonight, I forgot.

This isn't Montana where it would be pitch black outside as soon the sun sets. Here, there's usually a plethora of light coming from the cars, the street lamps, and other people's apartments across the way.

Still, ever since the incident, those lights weren't enough. I needed to keep the darkness out completely by closing the blinds. That is, until tonight.

An unfamiliar calmness settles over me.

This is the feeling that I have to remember when things get bad again.

It's not television but writing that has the capacity to soothe me like nothing else.

* * *

AFTER MAKING MYSELF A SALAD, I text Julie a picture of it.

LOOK! I'm not just subsisting on cereal anymore!

SHE TEXTS BACK three thumbs up and I sit down at the table to eat.

As I take the first few bites, my thoughts return to Jackson.

He is only a few years older than I am and a self-made billionaire, according to the Google net worth estimator, but who knows how accurate they are.

At the very least, he is very comfortable.

I wonder what that would be like for a moment; to not have any money worries.

What would I think about?

What would I do?

Do what you would do if you had a million dollars.

Isn't that what they always tell you when you're growing up?

Apparently, that's the metric for finding out what you would do for a living if money was no object.

Well, for me, it's simple.

I would write.

But what?

No, not these content writing pieces that I've been doing to make ends meet.

And not editing other people's resumes and cover letters.

No, I would write a book.

A love story.

But I can't really do that, can I?

I mean, it has always been my dream to write a novel, and I've made a number of attempts, some of them were quite serious.

With one, I even got to about halfway.

But then I couldn't figure out where to take them next.

The following morning, with newfound energy, I decide to return to my job search.

I need a job.

A real job.

I take out my phone and scroll through the various freelance writing websites that I have grown to rely on.

Most of the positions I have already applied for.

And the others either pay way too low or have very little steady work, making them hardly worth an application.

Julie keeps insisting that I give waitressing a shot again since whatever happened the first night that I tried it isn't the usual fare.

But for now, I just want to stick to what I know.

The thought of going outside at night, let alone dressed in a short dress, and getting into a stranger's car again after three a.m., just makes me sick to my stomach.

Hmm, what's this?

This is new.

Somebody is hiring a research assistant for an undisclosed project.

I focus on the word discreet.

Why would discretion be important?

There are only two types of people who would use that word; those involved in sex they don't want others to find out about, and the wealthy.

Because people looking to have secret liaisons

aren't likely to need a research assistant, I focus on the latter.

I read the job announcement again.

I'm a perfect fit.

Bachelor's degree in humanities.

Years of experience in writing on a variety of topics.

I make a few changes to my cover letter to tailor it to this position and submit it along with my standard resume via email.

I don't expect to hear anything back for a few days, but much to my surprise, a few hours later, I get a reply asking me when I can come in for an interview.

I write back immediately.

Another moment later, I get another email asking if I'm available this afternoon at four.

Wow, I must've made an impression.

I try to tread carefully so that I don't get myself all excited, the pay for this job is astronomical, but I can't help but feel giddy.

I jump into the shower, do my hair, and put on makeup.

It would be nice to go out and buy something new to wear to the interview, but I don't have the money.

So, I decide to just go with my go-to interview outfit.

A black skirt that I got at a second-hand store, a pink blouse, and a blazer that is supposed to match the skirt, but is a little bit off in its hue.

This will have to do.

Besides, it's a writing and researching job, right?

It's not like I'm a saleswoman.

About an hour and half before the interview, I decide to Google the address they gave me.

Oh my God.

No, no, no.

My hands start to shake as memories of what happened there flood my mind.

This can't be right.

This is the address of Jackson Ludlow's house!

CHAPTER 20 - HARLEY

WHEN I GET ANGRY...

I sit back in shock.

Is this a joke?

Does someone think that this is a funny thing to do to me?

Given what I've gone through in there.

Who would do this to me?

My mind runs through all the possibilities, but none of them are particularly realistic.

The guy who attacked me is currently sitting in jail awaiting trial.

The detective told me that she would call if they let him out on bail, and I haven't heard anything yet.

So, if it's not him, then who?

I don't have any enemies.

Julie is pretty much my only friend.

I'm not a particularly social person and I doubt that more than a handful of people in this city even know my name.

What if it's not a prank on me?

What if it's a prank on Jackson?

Given his wealth and stature, I'm pretty sure that he has made his share of enemies.

But what would be the point?

I think about that for a moment.

And then something else occurs to me.

What if it's Jackson who is doing this?

What if he's the one playing a joke on me?

I shake my head.

This just makes me angry.

Why?

What did I ever do to him?

Does he think this is funny?

He knows who I am.

He knows my name.

He invited me for an interview.

That is, if it was him who posted it.

I feel dizzy running over all the possibilities and not coming up with one concrete answer.

The problem is that there is no way to know what is going on here unless I go over there.

But why would I?

Now that I know that this whole thing is just one big prank.

I pace around my apartment trying to decide what to do.

I should stay home.

I should just not show up.

But the fact that someone even tried to do this to me makes me angry.

The girl from yesterday or a few days ago would just let this go.

She'd write it off as something shitty that happens.

But not now.

I feel invigorated.

Energized.

And mad.

I grab my purse and decide to get to the bottom of this one way or another.

***

I'm not ready to get into another car, so I take the subway and walk.

Twilight is falling, and I hate that I will have to get home in the dark but try not to think about that.

Instead, I look around at the beautiful tall trees that graze the street as the apartments get bigger and more spacious.

I try to focus on how beautiful this street is rather than what happened to me here.

Finally, I reach his house, exactly at four.

Without lingering for a moment, I walk right up the stairs and ring the doorbell.

If he makes me wait again, I'm going to walk away, I promise myself.

But I know that I won't keep it.

I'm going to ring that damn doorbell and pound on the door until someone opens and tells me what's going on.

"Hi."

The door swings open wide and a man dressed in an immaculately tailored suit opens the door.

His voice is smooth and welcoming.

But whatever anger I had building up within suddenly bursts out.

"What the hell is going on?"

"I needed to see you."

That answer takes me by surprise.

This isn't a prank at all?

This isn't a joke?

"You! You are the one who made up that job application!"

"Please come inside."

"No, I won't. I came here because I thought that

someone very cruel was playing a joke on me. Or maybe you. But I did not think that it *would* be you."

"This is not a joke. Nothing about this is a joke."

I shake my head in disbelief.

I want to turn around and walk away, but I also want to understand.

"Why? Why did you invite me here?" I demand to know, practically shrieking.

I am losing what little control I had left.

My body is shaking, partly from the cold, but mostly from the anger and anxiety that's building within me.

"Like I said, I needed to see you," he says calmly.

His voice is like velvet and that makes me even more mad.

"What do you mean?"

Why won't he explain more?

I take a deep breath and wrap my arms around my shoulders.

I hop from one foot to another to get some circulation going, but I haven't felt my toes for a few blocks.

"Please come inside. It's freezing out."

I want to protest, but with the wind picking up, my hands are so cold, they're getting little needles in them.

"I needed to apologize to you for how I acted before," he says, closing the enormous twelve-foot door behind me.

The foyer is grand and decorated in a tasteful modern style, which still keeps the features of its original design.

The chandelier is massive, but contemporary with what looks like a thousand naked bulbs.

But instead of producing a cold, sterile light, they bathe the room in the warm light of a candle.

To the right is a sitting room with a roaring fire with two, low, mid-century style sofas positioned on either side.

They are separated by a mismatched, but complementary coffee table.

The fireplace itself is similarly large and grand with an elaborate, and probably authentic, mantel above which hangs an enormous modern mirror.

Jackson shows me to the sofa on the right and then offers me a drink.

"I'm fine," I say.

"Please have a drink with me."

"Fine. I'll have a vodka with a splash of sparkling water and a slice of lemon."

He walks over to a carved cabinet, twice the size

of my dresser, and starts pouring liquids from different crystal vases.

The top of the cabinet is granite and it's embellished with antique brash finish hardware and multi-arched framed details.

Handing me my drink, he says, "Let me explain."

CHAPTER 21 - HARLEY

WHEN HE EXPLAINS...

The warmth of the fire feels nice on my body.

I take a sip of my drink, enjoying the feeling of the alcohol running through my veins, warming me from the inside out.

I resist the urge to unzip my coat and take off my hat and gloves.

"Can I take your jacket?"

"No, I'm not staying," I say stubbornly, even though by this point I am getting a little too warm.

"You said you were going to explain, so explain," I say, inching back a little from the fire.

Jackson adjusts himself a little on his sofa.

As he moves, his hair falls in his face, and he lets it stay there.

His hair is dark, rich, and curly in places.

It frames his face perfectly, accentuating his strong jaw and his Roman nose.

None of these things diminish the anger I feel toward him, but they do make him nice to look at.

"I wanted to ask you here to apologize for how I acted the last time I saw you. You were just thanking me, but I was rude. And I shouldn't have pushed your foot out like that."

I shrug, not knowing how to respond.

"I'm sorry. I am really sorry for that. I had my reasons, but that doesn't matter. I shouldn't have acted that way."

"I appreciate that," I say after a moment. "But why did you have to make up this job position? Why didn't you just call?"

He takes a moment to answer.

"I wanted to see you in person."

"Why didn't you just come to see me then?"

He takes a beat. "I couldn't."

I want to ask more; I get the feeling that this is already very difficult for him to admit.

"I wasn't sure if you would come if I came out and asked you directly."

"So, you just made this up?"

He shrugs.

"Don't you know that I'm looking for a job? I mean, I really need a job. And $50 an hour is a lot. Fuck, I should've known it was a scam," I say, finishing my drink.

I decide to make a swift exit, partly because I'm still angry at him, but mostly because I'm getting quite overheated and to take anything off would mean that I would be making myself comfortable.

But I slam the glass on the table a little too violently and it shatters in my hand.

"Oh my God! I'm so sorry," I mumble as I watch blood drip from my hand onto the shattered glass.

Jackson acts quickly.

He grabs a hand towel from the drink cabinet and takes my hand in his.

He carefully checks it for pieces of glass before wrapping it in the towel and lifting it above my head.

My head is spinning.

I am so hot that I feel like I'm going to pass out.

Yet, all I can do is mumble "I'm sorry" over and over again until Jackson takes his index finger and presses it to my lips.

"You have nothing to be sorry for," he whispers into my ear in his cool, calm voice.

Then he begins to undress me.

First, he carefully unwraps my scarf.

CHARLOTTE BYRD

It's long and wrapped three times around my neck.

He unspools it until my neck is exposed and I can breathe a little easier.

Next, he unzips my coat.

He tugs at the zipper and then pulls it all the way down.

With slow, yet meticulous movements, he pulls my unharmed arm out of the sleeve, keeping the other one elevated above my head.

Initially, I try to resist, but he firmly puts me back in place.

Then he lets my other arm down gently, takes off my coat, and pulls my arm back up into position.

The firmness of his actions sends shivers of excitement down my spine. I am in awe of how quickly he has taken control of my body.

Once my body is free of its outer clothing, Jackson turns his attention to my face.

He looks straight into my eyes, with his piercing intense eyes, before pulling off my hat.

Then he reaches down, smoothing my hair until every last strand is back in place.

For a moment, his gaze focuses on my lips.

Worried that they might be chapped since my

mouth feels like a desert, I run my tongue over my lower lip and then bite down a little.

And with that, he swiftly turns away from me and the moment is gone.

We were seconds away from kissing, but suddenly the mood has changed.

He walks over to the drink cabinet and pours us another round of drinks.

I sit here alone wondering if I have done something wrong, or whether I have completely made up this moment in my head.

But I do not dare ask.

"I need to get the emergency kit to fix up your hand," he says after taking a sip of his drink and handing me mine.

"No, thank you."

"It's in the bathroom down the hall."

I look up at him. He really doesn't get it.

"I meant, no thank you for the kit. I'm going to go home."

"But your hand might still have glass in it."

I shrug, grabbing my coat, scarf, and hat.

"I'm sorry, okay? I'm really sorry for...*everything*."

His voice is tense, loud, and full of emotion.

"Listen, I'm really fucked up. And I haven't dealt with people in a very long time."

"What do you mean?"

He takes a deep breath, as if he's gathering his strength.

"Until that night when you showed up at my front door, I haven't talked to another human being in real life for close to four years. That's why I'm a little...rusty."

He takes another deep breath.

When his eyes meet mine, he doesn't blink or look away.

I can sense that whatever he is telling me is the absolute truth.

"I shouldn't have made up that position, but I needed to see you. And I was afraid that you wouldn't come otherwise. I know it was..."

His voice trails off.

I fill in where he left off.

Inconsiderate.

Selfish.

Egotistical.

"I know that it was inconsiderate. Of you and your time. I just wanted to see you again. And not just to apologize. You are the first person I've wanted to see in a very long time."

I nod as if any of this makes sense.

"Listen, you don't want to listen to my bullshit.

But let me fix your hand. It's the least I can do. And then I won't bother you again."

The idea of heading home on the subway with a bleeding hand wrapped up only in a towel isn't particularly appealing.

Reluctantly, I agree.

CHAPTER 22 - HARLEY

WHEN HE MENDS ME...

I follow Jackson through the sitting room, and then the living room, toward the large guest bathroom near the kitchen.

Each room in this mansion seems to be bigger than the last, and the kitchen and the adjacent dining area are particularly spacious.

The ceilings here are even higher than they were in the foyer, with skylights and recessed lighting.

The bathroom is about half the size of my whole studio with a standing glass shower and a beautiful modern vanity.

In the cabinets next to the mirror, Jackson finds a first aid kit.

He sits me down on the lid of the toilet, taking my hand in his.

The lights are bright here and overhead, but he still looks as handsome as ever.

After removing his jacket, he carefully unwraps the towel around my hand and kneels down for a closer look.

He opens one of the individually wrapped, sterile gauze pads and pours some hydrogen peroxide on it.

Then he presses it to my hand.

There's one long cut down the side, but it's thin and the bleeding has already stopped.

Still, the cut bubbles and burns a little from the peroxide and I wince from the pain.

Jackson smiles out of the corner of his lips.

"I'm kind of a baby when it comes to pain," I explain even though that's pretty obvious.

"That's what I'm here for."

After he's satisfied that the wound is clean, Jackson opens an adhesive bandage and presses it on.

"According to my expert medical opinion," he says jokingly. "I think you'll live."

I take my hand back and again our eyes meet. Only this time, I'm not the one who looks away first.

"Well, thank you...for everything," I say when we walk back into the kitchen.

"Hey, are you hungry?"

I pause for a moment.

"I have some leftovers from last night here in the fridge. Nothing fancy. I'd love for you to join me."

The nonchalantness of the request catches me by surprise.

But without waiting for my answer, he opens the double door refrigerator and starts to lay out all sorts of goodies on the enormous sparkling- quartz kitchen island.

As I go back and forth on what I should do, I admire the French door refrigerator with wooden paneling that's a perfect match to the rest of the kitchen.

It makes the room look cohesive, elegant, and magazine-perfect.

"What do you say?" Jackson retrieves a large pan from one of the lower cabinets of the island.

When he leans over, I let my eyes linger on the muscles that contract and protrude through his dress shirt.

A part of me wants to leave right here and now, but a bigger part wants me to stay.

I don't exactly know why, except that something is pulling me closer to him.

"I guess that's the least you can do," I say with a smile.

Jackson heats up our food on the stove and makes a nice kale and arugula salad to go with his Indian food leftovers.

As soon as it's ready, I immediately reach for the saag paneer and finish what's left of it before he even gets a bite.

"That's not very nice."

"I'm not a very nice person. Besides, this is amazing."

"I know, that's why I ordered it."

I shrug and reach for some more rice.

"You are really making yourself quite at home," he points out with a crooked smile.

I look around his house and ask him about it.

Apparently, it was built by one of the wealthiest people in New York at the turn of the century.

And it stayed that way for a very long time, being saved, numerous times, from overzealous investors who wanted to buy it and break it up into apartments.

"Well, it is quite massive," I point out. "You don't think it's too big for one person?"

"I didn't buy it for one person."

There's a tinge of pain in his eyes when he says it.

I want to know more, but I don't feel like this is quite the right time.

So, I change the conversation by making a joke.

"You know you owe me a job."

I'm not a particularly forward person, but the words just spill out of me all at once.

I run my fingers over my glass and I realize that he has just refilled it.

Again.

That means I'm on my third drink, and that's way over my limit.

"How's that?" Jackson asks, laughing.

"Well, you tricked me into coming all the way over here. Wasted my time, and my time is valuable, you know."

My speech is getting tired and slurred, but I keep talking.

"I may not have a mansion like this, but I do have a studio apartment and no roommate anymore. And guess what? Not that many people want to move into an overpriced room with a total stranger. Even in New York!"

"I'm sorry about that," he mumbles, taking another bite.

"So, how about it?"

If I weren't drunk, I would never have the courage to demand a job.

But suddenly, I don't feel any shame in asking for what I want.

"You want a job?"

"No, let's get something straight. I *need* a job. Those are two very different things."

"What kind of job do you want?"

"The one I applied for sounded nice. And the pay did, too."

He thinks about it for a moment while I tap my fingers on the granite countertop impatiently.

For a second, I have an out-of-body experience where I briefly leave this scene and float up and watch myself from a distance.

Who is this girl? I wonder.

I mean, who the hell does she think she is?

"Okay, yes, let's do it," Jackson says, extending his hand. "You're hired."

CHAPTER 23 - HARLEY

COMPLICATIONS...

Wait a second, what just happened here?

I was just joking.

Is he joking?

The conversation drifts to another topic and soon dinner is over.

He offers to call me a car, but I prefer to take the subway.

"Thank you for staying and having dinner," he says, handing me my coat.

"Thank you for having me."

I put on my scarf and hat and zip up my coat.

When I open the door, a cold burst of air slams into my face and I pull the scarf tighter around my neck.

"Can you start Monday?" Jackson asks.

I turn around, confused.

"What do you mean?"

"Come at ten. I'm not much of a morning person."

"Wait, for what?"

"Your job. You still want to work, right?"

I hesitate for a moment.

"I thought you were just kidding."

"I wasn't. Were you?"

I shrug.

"You still need a job, right?"

I nod.

"Well, this one pays fifty bucks an hour. The hours are ten to six with an hour off for lunch at one."

"And what will I be doing?"

"Research. Writing. Not sure yet, but I have plenty of work for you to do."

I smile out of the corner of my mouth.

"Okay, I'll see you on Monday at ten."

* * *

THE ONE GOOD thing about the cold is that it tends to sober you up a bit and clear your head.

I wrap my arms around my body and brace myself against the whistling wind.

Did that just happen?

The same thought swirls around in my mind.

Am I really going to work for him? Did he really just hire me?

I do some quick math in my head.

Even if he doesn't pay me for my hour break for lunch, and I work seven hours a day, I'll get paid $350 a day!

Is that right?

I don't trust my calculations, so I pull out my phone to make sure that I did it right.

Yes, that's right.

So, that will be $1750 for the week!

Oh my God!

That's seven grand for the month.

If I work there a month, I will make seven thousand dollars!

I walk into my apartment on cloud nine.

I want to tell Julie, but I'm afraid of making this whole thing disappear.

I should go to bed, but I am too wired to sleep.

I'm not hungry and I'm definitely not into watching anything.

No, I'm not going to tell her what happened.

But I do have to share the news somehow.

I sit down and open my journal and do the only thing that feels right, I start writing.

I write about everything that happened without sparing any details.

I remember the way the wood crackled in the fireplace and the way that the room smelled of pine and whiskey.

I remember the way the shadows bounced off his face and wrapped around his strong jaw as he kneeled down and handed me my drink.

And the way the muscles of his body moved under his dress shirt.

The words flow out of me and I quickly fill close to ten pages in my barely legible scrawl.

But I know what I've written and I only stop when my hand can't continue anymore.

After pushing the pen into the paper to mark the end of the last sentence, I take a deep breath and close the journal.

I had forgotten how good it feels to write again.

But my reveling in the moment comes to an abrupt stop when my phone goes off.

I look at the screen.

It's from Detective Richardson.

What does she want?

"I'm sorry to call you so late."

"It's fine," I mumble. "What's going on?"

"Well, I promised to let you know what happened."

I wait for her to continue, holding my breath.

"Unfortunately, he was just granted bail. He will be released at seven in the morning tomorrow."

My whole body grows tense, and a few drops of cold sweat run down my spine.

My airway closes up and I feel like I can't breathe.

I freeze in place.

"Harley? Hello?"

"Yeah, I'm here."

"Listen, this isn't the optimal result, but it is what it is. He's out on bail but he can't come see you. That would be a violation of his bail."

"But what if he doesn't care? What if he comes anyway?"

"Then call the police. I have to go now. I'll keep you updated on what else happens."

She hangs up before I can ask anything else.

I don't know what else to do but call Julie and freak out.

She listens patiently and then tells me to calm down.

"You have until tomorrow morning, right?"

"Yes, but then...what if he comes here? I mean, I don't know if he knows our address, but I wouldn't be surprised."

Julie knows the story and she knows how serious this is.

I have a real reason to be afraid.

"If he found me there, he will find me...anywhere."

My words are rushed and out of control.

My whole body is shaking.

I don't know what to do to make it stop.

Tears are running down my cheeks.

"Okay, let's do this. Logan is out of town for awhile. Why don't you come here? There's no way he knows where I live. And then you'll be safe."

I think about that for a moment.

That could be a good option.

"C'mon, pack some stuff and come here. Bring enough that you won't have go back for at least two weeks."

"That sounds...perfect. But I don't want to impose."

"You won't be. It's just me and Mercury here. You'll have your own room. C'mon! It will be fun. I miss you."

"I miss you, too."

She's right.

Of course, she's right.

It's not like I have that many options anyway.

I can't afford a motel, not a New York City one, not even a Montana one.

And I don't really have any other friends besides her. But still, I don't want to be a burden.

"I don't know," I say after a moment. "Maybe I'm overreacting. Maybe he won't come here."

Julie takes a beat.

"If you don't come here yourself, I'm going to come there and pick you up. But you're coming over here one way or another."

CHAPTER 24 - HARLEY

WHEN I HAVE TO TELL THE TRUTH...

I arrive at Julie's new place an hour and a half later, dragging my large suitcase behind me.

My shoulders ache from my overstuffed tote and purse.

"Is that all you brought?" Julie asks in all seriousness when I come in.

She isn't exactly a light packer.

She takes the suitcase away from me and rolls it toward the couch, then she gives me a tour of the place.

The apartment is spacious with large floor-to-ceiling windows.

The decor is modern, and everything seems to be in black and white.

"I know what you're thinking. What the hell was he thinking, right?" Julie jokes, pointing to the black and white leather couch in the middle of the room.

"I didn't even know they made things like this."

"I'm going to be redecorating soon, but we still have to settle on a budget."

I smile.

"What? What is that?"

"Settle on a budget? You've become so domestic."

She laughs and shows me to my room.

The guest room is pretty large and decorated completely in white with accents of pink.

It doesn't make sense until Julie explains that's where his mother stays when she comes for a visit, so she decorated it herself.

After dropping off my stuff in my new room, I follow Julie into the living room.

"Tell me everything."

I fill her in on the details, as far as I can tell.

She listens carefully, shaking her head.

"I don't know what I'm going to do," I say, shaking my head.

She takes my hand in hers.

Up until this point, I've tried to put what happened out of my mind.

But now that he's out, I can't do that anymore.

"Did you tell the cops about him? I mean, do they know the whole truth?"

"I've tried to get a restraining order before, remember?"

"Yes, but this is different. He actually attacked you."

I nod.

I have to tell them.

Of course, I do.

I know that.

That guy isn't just some stranger off the street who one night decided to come after me.

No, that was a well-orchestrated plan.

"I know that you don't want to talk about it, Harley. I know. But you have to."

I nod.

She's right.

Of course, she is.

Besides, I'm the victim here.

He's the one stalking me.

And yet, like all victims, I feel shame.

I feel like I brought this on myself.

It's ridiculous, unfair, and unkind, but even now I have a hard time admitting how he became my stalker in the first place.

"You need to get a proper restraining order. You

need to tell the detective the truth," Julie urges.

Yes, but in order to do that, I would have to admit the truth to myself.

* * *

THE FOLLOWING morning I meet Detective Richardson at the precinct.

I expect to be taken into one of those little rooms where all things happen in the movies, but much to my surprise, she pulls over a chair next to her desk.

She's in the middle of lunch and offers me half of her sandwich, but I turn it down.

"So, what is it that you have to tell me?" she asks.

I stare at her glossy chestnut hair.

It's cut in a bob and it frames her face in a very attractive way.

She is wearing minimal makeup, and her lips are large and outlined in bright red lipstick.

Frankly, she's pretty enough to be a detective on television, not just in real life.

"It's okay, take your time," she says, putting her food down and taking a sip of her drink.

There's something very comforting in her demeanor and that helps me open up.

Even though I don't really have a choice.

Julie is waiting for me in the lobby, and her sole purpose in being here is to make sure that I actually go through with this.

"I wanted to come here in person to tell you a bit more about Parker Huntington."

She raises her eyebrows.

"You see, he's not just some random guy whose car I got into."

"I thought that you ordered a ride-share. Don't they assign random drivers that are closest to you?"

"Yes, I did. And he had a different name listed. But the thing is that it wasn't random. I mean, he didn't just decide to attack me once I got into his cab."

She narrows her eyes.

"Parker has been stalking me for awhile."

I pause to take a moment to gather my thoughts.

"Is he an ex-boyfriend?" she asks.

"No."

She waits for me to explain, but suddenly I don't have the strength to continue.

"Harley?"

"You see awhile ago, I ran this blog. It was my friend Julie's idea. She read one kind of like it, we both did. I'm a writer. Or aspiring writer. Whatever you want to call it. So, I thought it would be fun to do something like that, too."

"What kind of blog was it?"

"A sex blog. Basically, I pretended that I was an escort and I would describe all of my escapades and crazy things that happened on my dates. But the thing was that it was all fake. I made it all up. Every last encounter."

Detective Richardson nods for me to continue.

I take a deep breath and tell her everything from the beginning.

"It got to be pretty popular as far as blogs go. I had a pretty high readership. And I got a lot of emails from fans. Parker Huntington was one of those people. At first, he started writing me about how much he liked reading my stories. But then he started emailing me all the time. When I stopped writing him back, he got angry. Malicious even. He started sending me threats, so I blocked him. I thought that was it. But it wasn't. He hired a private investigator and found out my real name. And that's when he started showing up places where I was."

CHAPTER 25 - HARLEY

WHEN I TELL HER EVERYTHING...

y words start to come out all
at once.

I trip over them and continue to get the story out
as fast as possible.

"I didn't know who he was at first. He would just
sort of be there. At Starbucks. At the grocery store.
At the bookstore. And then he stopped trying to hide
in the shadows. He would just come up to me. At
first, he was friendly and kind of awkward. We
chatted a few times, but then he started to creep me
out by just being all of these places where I was.
Well, I stopped going outside that much. And one
time, I had to make an emergency run to get
something last minute. I thought for sure he
wouldn't be there, but he was. He walked up to me

and said, 'You're the whore who wrote Tangled Up. Well, I'm onto you, bitch. Why the hell are you ignoring me?'"

That's when I realized that he was Parker Huntington, the same guy who stalked me online.

That's when everything made sense and I started looking for work exclusively online.

It didn't pay as well as a regular job, but I couldn't bear the thought of going around the city knowing that someone was out there watching me.

And I couldn't bear to leave the city either.

I felt trapped.

Detective Richardson listens carefully, taking a few notes on her notepad.

"So, you were never an escort?" she asks.

"No."

"I need you to know that it's totally fine if you were. You won't get in trouble. I just need to know the whole truth, Harley."

Of course, she would think that.

Who else would write a sex blog?

But the truth is a lot less juicy than that, and actually a lot more pathetic.

"Please tell me, Harley."

"It was all made up. I promise you that. I didn't

have any of those experiences. I just have a very active imagination."

Detective Richardson nods her head, but doesn't look convinced.

"Okay, fine. You want to know the truth?"

"Yes, of course."

"I've never had any of those experiences because... I'm a virgin."

She stares at me in disbelief.

In a city, where having sex on a first date is practically expected, I'm a unicorn.

And that's not a good thing.

I shrug and wrap my arms around myself.

I feel so pathetic.

I'm almost twenty-six years old and I have the sexual maturity of a sixteen-year-old.

"Okay, I'm..." she stops herself from saying she's 'sorry' and instead corrects herself to say, "I understand."

"Everything I wrote about in there was made up. It was just for fun. And when people started reading it, it was exciting. I couldn't wait to make up more stories with bigger stakes and escapades."

"Is your blog still up?"

I shrug and nod.

I haven't written anything new in about two years, when he first started threatening me.

I couldn't really block him from reading it so I had to block myself.

I don't know if this was the right thing to do, but it felt right at the time.

Whenever I sat down at the computer, I felt his threats and presence looming over every word that I typed.

"It's still up. I never took it down."

She asks me for the web address.

She types it into the search bar.

"You're going to read it right now?" I ask, horrified.

"I'm just going to check it out a bit."

I cringe and ball up my fists.

The last post isn't that bad, I remember.

But instead of reading that one, she clicks on the side bar for one under the "most popular" category.

Shit.

The first one to appear is a gem, of course, I think to myself sarcastically.

HE LATCHED ONTO MY NIPPLES. "Careful there," I say, guiding his hands down my body.

"Tell me something you fantasize about," he instructs.

Without missing a beat, I say the first thing that comes to my mind.

"I'm abducted by four men, stripped, and tied up. They park and congregate around me, filling every part of me with them."

"I need more details," he moans.

"PLEASE STOP READING," I say, placing my hand on the screen. "I can't watch you read that."

"This is pretty graphic stuff," she states the obvious.

"It's a sex blog. It has to be."

She shrugs.

I hate the flash of something that I see in her eyes.

Is she judging me?

Really?

"What? Do you think I had this creep coming? You think it's my fault?"

"No, of course," she says definitely. "I'm sorry, I didn't mean to imply anything by saying that it was graphic. I wasn't judging you."

"Sure sounded like it."

"Okay, let's regroup. I will take a look through

this on my own time. Just for building the case. And I need you to show me all of your email that you had from him as well."

I shake my head.

This was a terrible idea.

I shouldn't have come here.

I was feeling guilty enough about everything anyway.

I mean, I know that it's not my fault.

All I did was write some sexy stuff on the internet.

Some fantasies.

And most weren't even mine.

That's it.

There's a ton more stuff online that's way worse than this.

It's hard to explain what it's like to have someone throw this in your face.

I was just doing it for fun, for a bit of entertainment, and then this man came along and made it all about him.

I called myself a whore in jest.

I was pretending to be an escort.

I wanted to be an evolved, strong woman who was taking charge of her life and the words that other people used to demean me.

But when he started using that word, I just retreated into myself.

I couldn't write that anymore.

I was afraid.

I was angry.

I was mad.

At both him and me.

Still, the words refused to come and I just let the blog go.

And now, all of this time later, he is still haunting me.

Well, fuck him.

And fuck Detective Richardson if she doesn't believe me.

I get up to leave.

"Where are you going?" she asks.

"This was a mistake."

"Harley, wait." She runs after me. "No, it wasn't. I am here for you. I'm on your side."

She blocks my exit to the door.

The few people who are within earshot look up at us.

I walk around her and open the door.

"Harley, I can get you that restraining order. I just need to put the case together. Please. Wait."

I hesitate.

"I need just a few more details before I can take this to the district attorney."

Even if I'm angry with her, I still need to focus on what's important.

I need the restraining order.

I need him to stay away from me.

I've come this far.

I shouldn't let her rattle me.

I nod and follow her to her desk.

CHAPTER 26 - HARLEY

WHEN I GET WHAT I WANT...

Even though to get an order of protection in the state of New York, you just have to go to the local courthouse and fill out the paperwork with details of the abuse, it was a good decision to go and speak with Detective Richardson directly instead of keeping her out of the loop and going straight to the judge.

She's the one in charge of my assault case and the one who has direct contact with the district attorney.

Within a few hours, I was in front of a judge stating my case with the district attorney by my side.

The process went a lot more smoothly than I actually anticipated.

I've never been before a judge before, and I

wished that I had worn something a little more appropriate than yoga pants and a hoodie, but luckily none of that seemed to matter much.

The district attorney only briefly mentioned my blog and the origins of my stalking relationship with Parker Huntington, without going into any specific details.

Soon after that, I was granted a restraining order.

Julie gives me a warm hug and wants to take me out to celebrate.

I'm happy, too; of course I am.

But I'm not exactly in a celebratory mood.

I don't know where he is or what kind of mood he'll be in when they serve him with it.

No, actually, I do.

He will be angry at me.

And then what?

"Listen, this is going to go a long way to keeping him away from you," Julie says.

I shrug.

"You don't believe me?"

"Well, no, I mean, I do. I'm just not sure it's going to keep him away from me."

She wraps her arms around me again, this time squeezing me more to assure me than to congratulate me.

"I'm sorry, I shouldn't be so negative. This is a good step. We had to do this, right?"

She nods.

"And it's going to work."

She smiles.

I smile back.

Neither of the smiles are genuine or honest, but that's okay for now.

It's enough to keep me going.

To celebrate, we decide to stop by Trader Joe's for a few bottles of wine and some food to go along with it.

Among the usual fare of groceries, I treat myself to a few containers of corn and quinoa salad with cotija cheese, roasted poblano, and cilantro dressing.

For dessert, I opt for the twenty-seven-layer croissini, which is a combination of a croissant and a grissini, an Italian breadstick, and it's one of the most delicious things in the world.

When we get home, or rather to her place, we dig into our foods without even unpacking it and putting it onto plates.

She pours us two glasses of wine and we clink our glasses.

"I want to thank you for taking me to see the detective. I don't think I would've done it without you. No, I know I wouldn't have. And despite how much I didn't want them to know everything about *that*, they really needed to if I want him to go away."

Julie clinks her glass to mine again.

"You would've done the same thing for me," she says.

I smile.

Yes, she's right.

I would've.

Though I probably would've been a lot less patient with her than she was with me.

As she turns on the television and starts clicking through the channels trying to find something, my mind goes back to the one thing that I haven't told her about yet.

Jackson Ludlow.

And my new job.

"Wait? What?" Julie gasps as I launch into the story.

She listens carefully, her body almost salivating as I tell it.

"You are going to work for Jackson Ludlow!" she squeals in excitement. "Is he as hot as he is rumored to be? You know that he's a recluse, right? A recluse billionaire, living alone in a mansion overlooking Central Park. I mean, how fucking romantic is that?"

I shake my head. "It's not romantic because it's purely business. That's it."

"You're not even a little bit attracted to him?"

I think back to the way the shadows danced off his chiseled face.

The sparkle of his eyes.

The darkness that brooded just below it.

"Yes, yes, you are! Oh my God! I was just kidding, but *you're* not!"

My face turns crimson.

"And he must be into you as well."

"Nope. That he is not."

"C'mon." She rolls her eyes. "He created a ruse to invite you to his house all to apologize to you. And then he offered you a job?"

I shrug.

"I don't know. But I can't think of it that way. I really need this job. I mean, he's going to pay me fifty dollars an hour. Do you know how quickly I can pay off my medical debt and maybe even save up money for my rent getting paid that much? Not to even mention the fact that if I can work there for a bit longer, I may even have a chance at paying off my student loans. I do owe over a hundred thousand."

"Oh, c'mon, student loans aren't a pressing matter. You're on an income-based repayment plan."

"Still, it's a really good job. And not one that I have any intentions of fucking up with any romantic liaisons."

"You're so boring." She shakes her head, laughing. "So, what are you going to do there?"

I stare at her, a little taken aback.

Her question is so simple and obvious, without an ounce of pretense.

Yet, I have no answer for her.

What the hell was I thinking?

"You have no idea what you're going to do there?" Julie gasps and then bursts out laughing. "Are you kidding me?"

"I never asked."

"What if he wants you to do something...sexual? I mean, it is fifty bucks an hour and he's a hermit. How much sex could he have had recently?"

She's just joking, mocking me.

But her words hit close to home.

What if he wants that?

My heart sinks.

What if that moment we had wasn't romantic at all?

What if he's just after me for something carnal?

"Okay, okay, slow down there," Julie says, taking my head in between her palms.

She pulls me close to her.

"I can see those little wheels in your head going round and round. I was just making fun, that's it. I didn't mean anything by it, and I definitely didn't mean to freak you out. I don't think he's a creep. I'm sure it will all be very...professional."

I force myself to believe her.

I have to.

But when I get to his house at ten that morning, I can't help but have butterflies in my stomach.

CHAPTER 27 - HARLEY

MY FIRST DAY...

I take a deep breath and ring the doorbell. No one answers.

I ring it again.

Again, no one answers.

I check the time.

It's exactly when he told me to show up.

I knock on the door, but it's so massive that I barely make a sound loud enough to hear myself.

Finally, the door opens and I see a stranger in front of me.

It's definitely Jackson Ludlow, but he doesn't look like the Jackson Ludlow I met before.

The man before me takes my breath away.

He stands tall, dressed in a three-piece black suit.

His tie is lavish and modern, with sparkles of blue which complement his irises.

His eyes narrow as he welcomes me inside, leaving whatever warmth they exuded before somewhere in another time.

The man before me is shrewd, assessing, and self-assured.

My heartbeat quickens, and my breaths speed up to match.

In the gray glow of daylight, the sitting room, which looked so cozy and romantic the last time I was here, now looks austere and cold.

When Jackson leans toward me, I notice how good he smells.

It's not the forced smell of cologne or even the lighter scent of a shampoo.

No, it's something subtler and yet more powerful than that, and it makes my mouth water.

"Thank you for coming," he says slowly.

As he extends his hand, my eyes catch the twinkle of his diamond cufflinks which match the sparkle of his very expensive looking watch.

I place my hand in his. I am keenly aware of how cold and clammy it is, but not shaking his hand is not an option.

My pulse quickens as his hand tightens around mine.

His touch sends electricity through me, sending shivers up my spine.

For a moment, he remains motionless.

He looks me up and down, taking account of every part of me.

"Are you okay?"

His voice comes out smooth and rich, without a single rasp.

For some reason, it makes my whole body tighten.

A moment later, when I relax, I realize that his voice has actually made me aroused.

I lick my lips and notice how dry and flaky they've suddenly become.

"I'm fine," I mutter.

I start to sweat, and I pull off my hat and scarf.

But it's not enough.

I need to take off my coat.

But I don't know where to put it.

"Let me help you," he says, putting his hands on me and pulling it off with one swift motion.

He then walks me to the foyer closet and hands me a hanger.

"You can put all of your stuff here."

For a moment, I'm taken aback by the briskness of his actions.

But I also find myself strangely attracted to his seemingly ungentlemanly, or perhaps outright rude approach to inviting me into his home.

After I put away all of my stuff, I close the door and stand before him.

Our eyes meet and neither of us look away.

He looks younger than he did before, yet his eyes are worldly and knowing.

He has seen his share of heartache and darkness.

And there's something else in them, too.

Hard. Like ice.

As he stares into my eyes, I wonder what he sees in mine.

A moment passes and then another.

Finally, I am the first one to look away.

I feel myself drawn to him.

But it's not just his handsome face that pushes me toward him.

It's more than that.

He's not merely handsome; he is outright beautiful.

But beyond the physical, it's the damage and the darkness in his eyes that pull me closer as if he were a magnet.

It takes all of my strength not to reach up and press my lips onto his.

It takes even more of my strength not to run my hands over his chest.

I am shocked by the thoughts that run through my mind.

I've never felt this way before.

So...enthralled.

"Let me show you to your office," he says and waves for me to follow him. "Oh, how's your hand?"

"It's fine."

As he walks away, my eyes run down his broad, perfect shoulders and down his narrow waist.

They pause when they reach his butt. Pert and high and full of muscle, it's all I can do to not run over and grab it.

"You coming?" he asks, turning around in the doorway.

"Um, yes, of course."

My words come out hurried and frazzled.

They're a bit of a reflection of how I feel.

Why the hell did I have to tell Julie about any of this?

She was the one who planted these ideas in my head.

He doesn't like me.

And I shouldn't like him.

This job is too important to mess it up with something personal that will probably go nowhere.

And then...bang.

My knee catches one of the dining room chairs and I nearly topple over.

At the very last minute, I catch myself and straighten out.

"I'm so sorry," I say over and over again.

Oh my God.

I'm such a spaz.

What the hell is going on with me?

It's like when I'm around him, I completely lose control of myself.

"Are you alright?" he asks.

"I'm fine. I'm totally fine. Let's keep walking," I say, trying to make this moment end as quickly as possible.

The only problem is that it doesn't.

He is genuinely concerned about me.

"Maybe you should take a seat."

I shake my head no.

Then I start walking not very gracefully and with a significant limp.

After a moment of hesitation, he lets it go and

leads me through a large marbled hallway toward the last room on the right.

The door is a thick oak and swung open.

Inside, there's a spacious table, about the size of my twin bed growing up, and books lining each wall.

"This is where you'll be working. You brought your computer, correct?"

I nod.

I didn't know it was a requirement, but I tend to bring it everywhere I go.

"What is it exactly that I'll be doing?"

"I have a number of proposals that I receive everyday from prospective online magazines, blogs, and podcasts that are interested in joining Minetta. I assume you know what we're about. So, I want you to go through them and present to me the ones that you think will be a good fit. "

Present.

My throat closes up.

CHAPTER 28 - HARLEY

LATER...

*M*y hands get clammy.

My heart skips a beat and another one and another one.

"What...do...you...mean by present?"

"Nothing formal. Just tell me which you think one will be a good one for us to acquire and why."

I nod.

That sounds less formal, but no less scary.

"I already sent you an email with all the prospects."

I nod confidently.

I have embarrassed myself enough today and I can't make him think that I'm not up for the job.

"Besides this, I will need you to run errands.

Take packages. Pick up packages. Nothing too strenuous. Does that sound good?"

I nod.

"Okay, I will leave you now."

I go over to my desk and run my fingers over the grain.

The table is made up from one complete piece of wood and it's exquisite.

"One other thing, Harley. Never ever go into the upper west wing of this house. Not for any reason."

I nod.

"I need you to promise me and say that you understand that if you do, you will be terminated immediately."

His eyes narrow as he says that, almost as if he's challenging me.

His gaze fills me with restless energy and I agree to never go there out loud.

His lips curl a little at the edges, and I can see that he seems satisfied.

THE DAY PROCEEDS in a rather humdrum manner.

After he leaves, I never see him again.

The only reason I know that he's still here is that I know he doesn't leave this house.

This house.

This place isn't exactly a house.

It's a mansion.

I bet twenty people could live here without crowding each other much.

I take a break around one and head to the kitchen.

In the two hours that I've been here, I've managed to get a lot better acquainted with the type of material that Minetta Media puts out.

Instead of focusing on superficial, on the surface type stories about current events, their mission is to delve deeper.

For example, stories about the lack of affordable housing in the city focus on public policy decisions that have been made in the last half a century that led up to the current situation.

You wouldn't think that in today's world, where everyone conveys every thought in one hundred and forty characters, there would be much space for organizations that focus on in-depth analysis and reporting.

But in fact, there is.

A growing number of readers and listeners seem

to be craving this type of reporting and that's exactly why Minetta is doing so well.

From the list that he has sent me, I decide that two blogs and two podcasts are a definite great fit and another two are pretty good continuers if he ever wants to expand into something that's a little bit more pop culture.

Once I make these decisions, I type up a few notes about what I liked and disliked about each one to support my decision.

By the time I'm done, I feel completely sick to my stomach and decide to pull away from work for a bit and grab a bite to eat.

I'm not sure if I'm allowed to eat in the kitchen, but I brought my own lunch just in case I wasn't.

I wasn't sure how this day was going to go and wanted to be prepared with food reinforcements just in case.

After pouring myself a glass of water, I sit down with my paper bag lunch.

It's nothing special.

Just a salad I got from Trader Joe's last night along with a nut bar.

When I'm done, I'm satiated but no less worried.

The thing is that any type of public speaking gives me major anxiety.

My underarms are drenched in sweat.

The room is not particularly warm, and that makes things even worse.

The more I sweat, the colder I get, which makes me sweat even more.

I look under my cardigan.

There are large and ever-growing pit stains on top of my blouse.

Great.

Now, there's no way I'm taking this off today.

Just remember that being near Jackson gives you hot flashes, like it did before.

For a moment, I actually consider what I would do if he were to start kissing me right here and now and he wanted to take off my clothes.

No, I couldn't bear the humiliation.

No matter how much I want him, I would keep my cardigan on.

I roll my eyes at my ridiculousness.

I curse Julie for putting stupid ideas into my head and try to put him out of my mind.

Except that I can't.

Of all the words in the English language, why did he have to use the word *present*?

That's the one that makes me shake uncontrollably as my thoughts drift back to one

177

particular sixth grade presentation in social studies.

I was a really shy kid who preferred to keep her nose in a book rather than socializing with others.

But I don't remember having as much fear about speaking in public until after that day.

Everyone in the class was assigned to a week throughout the year when they had to do a presentation of what was going on in the news that week.

We had to design a poster and a short speech.

My parents were going through something that week, I can't quite remember what, but it made it difficult for me to ask them to take me to the store for poster supplies.

I had a poster from an old presentation I'd done for another class, so I just flipped it over and wrote some stuff.

I had glue but no construction paper or markers, so I wrote everything up in different colors of ink.

Most of the girls in the class went out with elaborate fold out posters with pockets and a million different kinds of decorations.

But that was the least of my problems that day.

The thing was that Oklahoma was in the news

that week and it took me forever to carefully write out and color in the word on the top.

But it wasn't until I stood in front of the class, with my speech written entirely on a piece of paper, that the boy in the front row laughed and pointed out the fact that I had misspelled Oklahoma with "Oc" in the front.

When he laughed, the entire class laughed, even the teacher.

Of course, he later said he wasn't laughing at me, just at my mistake, but the image of everyone laughing solidified in my mind and has stayed with me until this day.

CHAPTER 29 - HARLEY

WHEN I PRESENT...

After I finish my lonely lunch in the spacious kitchen, I decide to go upstairs.

Jackson told me not to go to the upper west wing of the house, but he didn't say anything about just going upstairs.

I ascend up the winding grand staircase.

My heels make a loud clinking sound with each step.

When I get to the top, I look over the foyer and the elaborate art-deco chandelier hanging from the ceiling.

It looks like it's almost suspended in space.

The view from the top is magnificent.

Grand in every way imaginable.

When I turn to my left, I see my reflection in the mirror.

Mousy.

A little too short and not exactly with the body of a model.

I know that everyone is now promoting self-love and I do love myself.

But I still can't help but feel not entirely comfortable in my skin.

My thighs are bigger than I think they should be, and my stomach isn't as flat as I would like it to be.

But looking at myself in the mirror here, in the middle of this red carpet with its perfect candlelight lighting, I suddenly see a different Harley.

Someone a lot prettier than the girl I remember seeing this morning in the mirror in my bathroom.

And with that, I stand up a little taller.

I extend my chin a little higher.

My shoulders straighten out.

And suddenly, I like how I look, a lot.

I even pull out my phone and take a selfie.

I do my best mirror selfie with my body contorted at angles so that I look my best.

I stare at the picture and am amazed by how good I look.

Is it just me or is this mirror amazing and ridiculously flattering?

Or maybe this is how I look in real life and my mirrors back home just suck.

Then something occurs to me.

What would make this moment even more perfect is if I weren't dressed in a business suit at all.

No, I should be standing here in a long, sparkling, floor length gown and heels that make me reach for the heavens.

Then...I'd be...wow.

"Harley?"

His voice emerges from the dark hallway.

I hide my phone behind my back and stand in front of him like a deer in headlights.

"I'm sorry. I was just...taking a picture."

I feel vapid and narcissistic.

And stupid. I'm pretty sure that he is well above posting pictures of himself on social media, but the truth is that I don't have too many good ones to post.

I never look that great and I never really do anything fun.

And this mirror is...amazing.

Still, I really don't want him to think I'm some social media obsessed bimbo.

"It's perfectly fine," he says in his silky, smooth voice.

"I was actually coming to find you. I think I narrowed down that list of podcasts and blogs you gave me."

"Let's go to the sitting room and we can go over them."

I follow him down the hall to another formal room, which looks a lot like drawing rooms do in the movies about people who live in big mansions.

Lots of couches, most of them look too antique to sit on.

A few chairs.

No television or anything a normal room would have.

Each wall is adorned by large-scale pairings which take up almost half the space.

He takes me to one side of the room where a few fabric chairs and sofas are arranged across from each other.

He sits in the large chair in the middle at the head of the coffee table.

"Okay, I'm all yours."

His choice of words throws me off guard.

I freeze for a moment.

When I finally come out of my daze, I debate

whether I should go sit down next to him.

I want to, but now I've been standing here so long that it feels a bit awkward to do that.

Oh, how I wish I had my laptop with me so I could hide behind it as I speak.

Suddenly, something occurs to me.

Of course.

I saved the document in my cloud, so I can access it with my phone.

I point to the phone and wait impatiently for the page to load.

Meanwhile, Jackson sits back in his chair with one leg crossed on top of the other at the knee.

His arms are swung casually around the arms of the chair and he looks relaxed.

In charge.

Completely comfortable.

His shirt is as starched and white as it was earlier today, without a single wrinkle.

His pencil-thin silver tie clip catches my eye and makes me blink from the glare.

His jacket falls open, but his shirt is buttoned all the way to the top with a perfect tie.

I jerk to a halt and notice that my page had loaded a long time ago.

When my eyes meet his again, I can see his

smiling.

Okay, I need to sit down, I say to myself. I can't stand here before him and give him an actual presentation.

I'm going to freak out.

This is just a casual chat, so why am I making this so formal?

I take a few steps toward the chair to his right, but he stops me.

"You can stay right there."

My chest closes up, but I force a breath in and out through the pain.

I take a step back to my previous location.

"You can start at any time," he says casually.

I look at the screen and then back up at him.

With each look, he appears to be even more striking than he did before.

His hair falls in large dark curls, but only in a few spots around his face.

They're actually more like waves, rather than curls, and they frame his face in that way only beautiful hair can.

Stop.

Stop staring at him, I say to myself.

And start talking.

I take another breath and open my mouth.

WHEN THINGS GO AS PLANNED...

"After researching Minetta Media a bit." My voice comes out a little weak, but after clearing my throat, I make my words more forceful.

"I've come to the conclusion that it mainly focuses on in-depth, policy analysis type reporting, whether it is in blog, article, or podcast form. That's your main focus."

Out of the corner of my eye, I see him nodding, but I don't focus on that.

I can't.

The only way I'm going to get through this is by reading what I had typed up earlier today.

"Well, given that, I thought that these ones were the best fit for Minetta at this point."

I dive into my analysis of each of the blogs that I had read earlier.

Everything that I say is written out and I turn my phone on its side to be able to read the whole page without scrolling or minimizing and maximizing all the time.

As I read, I see him smiling a bit, but I'm not sure if he is laughing at me doing this presentation the only way that I know how, or at the content of what I'm saying.

"Is there something funny?" I ask, right before I continue with my analysis of the podcasts that I'd chosen.

I meant to keep my mouth shut, but I can't do that any better than I can give a good speech.

"No, not at all."

"So, then you're just laughing at me? My presentation?"

Just be quiet.

He was listening.

Why are you making this about you?

"I was smiling because I was enjoying your presentation. I've never seen anything quite like it."

My cheeks turn beet red.

I turn off my phone.

"I'm not very good at public speaking, so what?

That wasn't the job you hired me for. You hired me to write and analyze and be your personal assistant. If you need someone who can give speeches, then you should go to someone else."

"There."

"What?"

"You just spoke a period of time, looking me straight in the eyes with your shoulders straight, and without your head buried in your phone."

I shrug.

"I'm just pointing out to you that you are capable of it. And I am sorry that someone, probably a long time ago, made you feel like you weren't. Because you are quite...extraordinary at it."

Extraordinary? Well, that's one way of putting it.

"I was just...angry."

"Maybe you should be angry more often."

I look down at my phone and lift it up to my face to start again.

"Wait a second," he says. "Give me that."

I freeze.

"Trust me."

I hand him my phone.

"Now talk."

I search my mind for what I was about to say next, but nothing comes to mind. I start to fidget.

"Come sit here."

Again, I do as he says.

"Now tell me. What did you like about Timothy Hartwick's podcast?"

I take a deep breath and try to focus.

"I need my phone. I can't do it without it."

"Yes, you can."

"You don't actually know that."

"Yes, I do."

I narrow my eyes.

Sitting this close to him, I realize that he is even more striking than I had previously thought.

His hair is shiny and glossy, and I clench my fists to resist the urge to run my fingers through it.

"Just...relax."

He places his hand on top of mine.

A shock of electricity runs through my body and is quickly followed by another and another.

If this is his attempt to make me feel more comfortable, it's not working.

"Now...tell me."

But I no longer have the ability to speak.

Whatever thoughts I had in my mind have completely vanished, and I feel like a complete fool.

He's going to think I'm stupid.

Tears are starting to well at the back of my eyes, and I rush to my feet to make them stop.

I make it across the room before he catches up with me.

My breathing is so fast that I'm about to have a panic attack.

I haven't had one since I was eight and got yelled at by my first grade teacher in front of the whole class.

But the tightening of my chest and the tingling of my fingers is undeniable.

It's either that or I'm having a heart attack.

"Here, let me help you," he says, taking my limp body into his hands.

He pulls me over to the nearest sofa, spreads my legs, pulls up my skirt a little, and pushes my head in between them.

"You are having a panic attack. Just take slow deep breaths and everything will be fine."

I do as he says, and after a few moments, my breathing does get better.

When I feel strong enough to lift up my head, I wipe the tears off my face.

They are not tears of sadness, but rather of anxiety.

I still feel like a massive fool for having a panic

attack in front of my boss, but I try not to think about that.

He pulls away from me and gives me some space.

"I guess you don't want me to come back tomorrow," I say after a moment.

He turns around, adjusting his perfectly knotted tie.

Please don't say yes.

Please don't say yes, I pray.

"Why would you say that?"

"Because I'm not very good at this."

"How about you just email me from now on?"

I nod and let out a big sigh of relief.

This presentation has gone as bad as it possibly could, and he must think that I'm the biggest spaz in the world, but at least I still have my job.

"C'mon, let's get something to eat."

I follow him back downstairs toward the kitchen.

When he grabs some juice from the refrigerator and offers me a glass, I take a moment to admire him.

Gorgeous.

Perfect.

At least, as far as his looks go.

I imagine how hard his body is under those clothes and then my thoughts drift elsewhere.

What would it be like to kiss him?

To run my hands down his stomach?

To grab his perfectly toned butt?

"So, what do you think of my company?" he asks casually.

"*I* actually really admire what you do. Not a lot of online sources go so deep into every aspect of the story. Public policy isn't the sexiest thing out there, you know."

"I've heard that before."

"I'm kind of surprised you have made it work so well and it has become so profitable."

"Oh, you checked my financial statements, did you?"

I shrug. "I know what I read in Fortune. You are almost a billionaire, right?"

"I am quite comfortable."

I laugh. "That's what people who have a lot of money always say."

"Minetta isn't my only company, but it's the one

closest and dearest to me. I started it on my own and it was the first company to really give me serious money."

"So, Fortune's assessment isn't accurate?"

"No, they are pretty close, but most of my wealth comes from a few strategic investments that I made in a few startups, which then went public."

I nod.

It makes sense, but his world is so far away from mine that I have a difficult time relating.

I decide to pivot the conversation to something I do know.

"There is one more podcast that I wanted to tell you about. I forgot the names of the producers, but they are out of Saint Louis. They have a show on the public housing situation there with really good in-depth interviews with both people living in those apartments, trying to get public housing vouchers and the landlords. Every few shows they also go back in time and compare what social changes led to the public policy being designed at the time, and how it evolved over time. But it's not dry at all. Not boring. They do a lot of personal accounts, which really bring you into the story. So, if you are in a position to make them an offer, you should really give them a chance."

He stares at me for a moment.

Then blinks and looks away.

"What?"

"It's amazing what we can accomplish if we don't feel the pressure to be perfect."

Yes, of course.

It suddenly hits me.

Without overthinking it, I just came out and told him exactly what he was asking me about before.

"While I'm at it, let me tell you some of my other thoughts on what I read and listened to today."

And with that, I delve into everything that I had written up so diligently earlier in the day.

I shut down my mind and any thoughts about what I look like or sound like as I talk and just let my words flow out of me.

This is not a presentation.

This is just a friendly chat.

I'm telling him what I think.

What's important are my ideas, nothing else.

When I finish, I take a deep breath and smile.

I am actually proud of myself.

Somewhere in there, I lost myself in the speech.

I no longer existed and what did exist were my ideas.

"Thank you for sharing your thoughts. I will take them under consideration."

I nod.

"Well, I guess I'll get back to work now. I haven't gotten through the whole list yet, and I want to make sure my recommendations are thorough."

He nods approvingly and watches me exit.

ONCE I GET to my office, I let out a big sigh of relief.

I am so proud of myself.

The words come from my heart and I didn't feel any anxiety while I was talking.

But after that, with his gaze on me, I couldn't handle it anymore.

I needed to get away.

I needed space to come to terms with everything that had happened earlier today.

I decide not to dwell on any of this any longer.

I still have my job.

I showed him that I'm not an idiot.

And that's enough for now.

I turn on my laptop and bury my attention in the links and articles that Jackson has sent to me.

As I read, more emails arrive from him with more blogs to look at.

At the end of each, he always says, no rush.

I take my time and carefully go through each one.

I don't know how to look up how many web clicks they have or how much readership they have each week, so I focus on the content.

Is this a good fit?

Or is it not?

At six p.m., I close my laptop and stretch out in my chair. I actually worked the whole time.

The thing is, that I find this work interesting and when it's something that I like then I tend to lose track of time very quickly as I bury myself in it.

I'm not sure if I should just leave and come back tomorrow or tell Jackson that I'm leaving.

I decide to go find him and let him know.

I head up the staircase and wander down the hallway from which he came before.

I find him in a large room with floor-to-ceiling windows overlooking the city on two sides.

To one side, there's a large desk, about twice the size of mine, which is covered with computer screens.

The door is open and I knock loudly.

Jackson is standing facing away from me with his face toward the cityscape.

His legs are spread out wide and he is talking loudly.

There's someone else on the phone.

I can hear their frantic typing as Jackson speaks.

He raises his index finger in the air to call me to his attention but continues to rattle off instructions to the person on the call.

I wait patiently.

When he hangs up, he turns to face me.

"It's six. I just wanted to let you know that I was going to leave."

"Okay, thank you." He nods.

His eyes don't focus on mine. Instead, he is lost somewhere in space.

"Is everything okay?"

"Um...yes," he says, distracted.

"Okay, I'll go then."

I turn around to leave.

I'm halfway down the stairs when he calls my name.

"What are you doing tomorrow night?"

I shrug. "Nothing, really."

"Will you accompany me to a black tie fundraiser?"

"Sure."

The word comes out before I can really think about it and immediately regret it.

A black tie event?

I don't have anything to wear.

And I don't have any money to buy something with.

"Great. You can work from home tomorrow if you want and take your time getting ready. I'll have a stylist come to your place with some dresses, shoes, and accessories to try on in the afternoon. A car will pick you up at 6:30."

And with that, he disappears upstairs.

CHAPTER 32 - JACKSON

WHEN SHE LEAVES...

*A*s soon as I hear her answer, I walk straight to my bedroom and let out a big sigh of relief.

I don't know what I would do if she had said no.

I pace in circles, feeling the outside of my suit.

It's my armor and in it I feel powerful and invincible.

What the fuck am I going to do? I roar inside of me.

Anxiety morphs into anger and rage.

The truth is that my companies are not doing that well.

I need a big infusion of cash, and fast, if I want to keep growing and I don't want to fire anyone.

No, expansion is the only solution.

I am not ready to let anyone go at this point, if there's another way.

And there is.

Phillips and a few other people at the top of the food chain at Minetta are urging me to take this meeting with Woodward.

He made a lot of money investing in solar on the West Coast and is now expanding into investing in startups and media organizations that are aligned with his interests.

I've never had to raise capital before and starting with Woodward is definitely starting at the top.

But if we can reach an agreement that we are both comfortable with, then it will allow me to keep running Minetta as I see fit without laying anyone off.

I can still hear Phillips' words in my head.

"You have to meet him in person. There are rumors that you're a bit crazy. Rich people can be eccentric, but they can't be crazy. Especially if they want someone like Woodward to invest in their company."

She's right.

I know that she's right even before she finishes talking.

I've read the articles.

I've seen the press.

I'm not a celebrity, so people weren't that interested at first.

But I am wealthy, so someone finally noticed that I haven't been seen at any events for a long time.

If I want to make a good impression, I need the world to see me out in public.

My thoughts drift back to Harley.

Her whole body was shaking from fear when she stood before me, but she still tried.

And it wasn't until after she had the panic attack that she actually gave up.

I admire her courage.

True courage isn't the absence of fear; it's doing whatever you are afraid of anyway.

THE FOLLOWING DAY, my tuxedo arrives and I try it on.

I get dressed, averting my eyes from the full length mirror in my bedroom.

It is only after the entire outfit is complete that I look at myself.

Tall.

Dark.

Handsome.

Is that how the cliché goes?

Well, that's me.

The tuxedo has tails and it fits perfectly, tailored to my measurements precisely.

The material is rich and luxurious and doesn't bulk up in any place.

It accentuates my waist and gives my ass a nice lift.

I look confident and pulled together.

I'm the poster child of what it means to be filthy rich and successful.

And yet, it's all a lie.

Inside, my body is screaming.

My heart is beating out of my chest and my palms are sweaty.

I clench my jaw to keep my thoughts away from the surface.

I am an actor.

I have to the play the part of Mr. Ludlow to perfection if I want this to work.

Elegant.

Suave.

And, of course, utterly charming.

The doorbell rings.

It's my driver.

I've never met him before, but his company is known for their discretion in the business and as a result they are often used by celebrities, diplomats, and businesspeople who appreciate that sort of thing.

"I'm Lester Garbo," he introduces himself as he opens the door of the BMW SUV with tinted windows for me.

"It's nice to meet you, Mr. Garbo."

"You can call me Lester, Mr. Ludlow."

"Only if you call me Jackson." I've never been one for formalities and prefer to use the title of Mr. in a more formal setting.

He takes a beat, thinking about the proposition.

"Oh, I couldn't do that," he finally says.

"Okay, then, Mr. Garbo, please drive me to the Lower East Side," I say, giving him Harley's address.

Driving down the rushing traffic streets of New York gives me a strange sense of calm.

I look out of the window at the flashing lights and the bustling crowds.

Some people are running to make their trains, others are walking slowly, their arms full of tonight's groceries.

A little boy and a little girl are dancing around

TANGLED UP IN ICE

their tired mother as she buys some vegetables from a stand.

The light turns green and we drive another block.

Here, a woman in a suit and white sneakers is walking, holding her heels in her hands.

A man walking his Labrador bends over to pick up his poop.

I never knew how much I would enjoy sitting here and simply driving down the streets.

I thought that being here would make me anxious, but it is, in fact, the opposite.

Why haven't I done this in so long?

"I'm sorry about that," Mr. Garbo says.

The car comes to a sudden stop after someone cuts us off, but even that doesn't faze me.

I look at the white lights which are sprinkled on one leafless tree and the way they twinkle in the night.

An old woman with an even older and smaller dog waits next to it for the dog to do her business.

Her face is serene and contemplative, and she doesn't seem at all put out by this inconvenience.

Looking at her gives me a bit of peace.

My hands relax fully and I am no longer grasping the hand rest in the back.

I sit back more in my seat and enjoy the ride.

Twenty minutes later, we arrive in front of her building.

Mr. Garbo double parks the car, since there isn't a parking spot in sight, and puts on his blinkers.

"No need. I'll get her," I say and get out of the car before he can protest.

I don't know if this is according to protocol, but nothing about me so far has been.

Plus, I don't give a shit.

CHAPTER 33 - JACKSON

WHEN I SEE HER AGAIN...

The doorman opens the door for me and welcomes me inside.

Then he calls her apartment and tells me that she will be down shortly.

I wait in the lobby.

The floor is made of marble and decorated with functional, but beautiful, contemporary furniture.

The theme seems to be white and gray, giving the place a very wintery feel.

This is the moment that I was certain I'd start to feel the claustrophobia set in.

I wait for my chest to tighten and my heartbeat to speed up, but nothing happens.

I'm amazed by how relaxed and almost on an even keel I feel.

The only thing that does make my heart jump, but in a good way, is the anticipation of seeing her again.

The elevator doors open and the wind gets knocked out of me.

Harley looks absolutely breathtaking.

She is dressed in a long, red, floor-length gown.

It's decorated with about a million little beads and gives her body a beautiful silhouette.

The v-neckline cradles her breasts and pushes them up to the sky.

The dress has thin straps and her collarbones are adorned with a thin diamond necklace, which I had requested that the stylist bring for her.

My eyes drift north.

Her shoulder-length chestnut hair falls in voluminous curls around her face and her hazel eyes twinkle.

Her lips are outlined in bright red, a perfect match to her dress, making her olive skin practically light up.

"You look...breathtaking," I whisper, almost unable to speak.

My heart skips one beat and then another, but it has nothing to do with being in public for the first time in a long time.

"Thank you." She looks me up and down. "You don't look half bad yourself."

She swings her scarf around her neck and I help her with her coat.

It's a black puffy coat, which isn't that puffy at all, but doesn't do well in complementing the dress.

"I wasn't sure if I should bring it, but it's like nineteen degrees outside. I didn't want to freeze."

"Of course. Here, zip it up." My hand reaches for the zipper, which starts near her thigh, and I pull it all the way up to her throat.

The zipper slides smoothly up her body, pausing only slightly as it pulls her breasts closer together. She inhales deeply and then exhales as I let go.

For a moment, I hesitate.

Did I overstep my bounds?

Did I make her uncomfortable by taking it a step too far?

But then she gives me a wide smile and a sense of relief sweeps over me.

"I really appreciate you coming with me tonight," I tell her when we pull away from the curb. "It's going to be a challenging evening for me."

"Why is that?"

Suddenly, it occurs to me that she may or may not know about that part of me.

I press the button and a dark privacy screen rises up between us and Mr. Garbo.

"I haven't been out in public for a very long time," I say after the screen goes all the way up and we have the utmost privacy.

"Actually, before you showed up on my doorstep, I haven't stepped foot outside my home in almost four years."

She gasps.

"It was a long time," I admit. "But the years seemed to have flown by. I got used to my way of doing things. That's why it took me so long to answer the door after you knocked."

"I'm sorry."

"No, please don't be. You crashed into my life and changed...everything. And that was a good thing."

She nods.

I lean over and pull her chin up so I can see her eyes.

They are almond shaped and tilted a little upward at the edges.

To say that they are beautiful would be the understatement of the century.

"I am not telling you any of this for you to feel sorry for me. I just want you to understand where

I'm coming from. This is my first public event in a very long time and I don't exactly know how it's going to go."

"I get the sense that you didn't get much of a say in whether you were going or not."

I avert my eyes from hers for a moment.

"Your senses are on point. I am meeting with a potential investor in Minetta and if we can come to an agreement then I won't have to lay off anyone."

She nods.

"That's what's important to me. The company isn't doing as well this quarter as we thought it would. And somebody has to pay. In this case, I'm choosing for that person to be me."

* * *

WE WALK into the Magellan Hotel on Central Park West and drop off Harley's outerwear at the coat check.

One of the people from the front desk shows us toward the fundraising event ballroom.

I am not entirely sure what this fundraiser is even raising money for, but that's the least of my worries.

My main concern is just the swarm of people that occupy the space.

The hotel's primary colors are gray, black, and silver with touches of white.

The men in their tuxedos blend into the background while the women with their long, elaborate gowns in all the colors of the rainbow stand out like peacocks.

The flashes of color overwhelm me.

They assault my senses and my body starts to tense up without my control.

Probably sensing that something is wrong, Harley takes me by my arm and leads me to the bar.

"Don't look at any of them. We are the only ones here. The only ones who matter. C'mon, why don't you buy me a drink."

Her suddenly taking charge of the situation puts me at ease.

I inhale slightly and my chest doesn't seize up in pain.

I take another one and another one.

The more oxygen that reaches my brain, the better I start to feel.

She orders me a whiskey and for herself she gets a vodka on the rocks with a twist.

This particular bar is one of five stations around the room and it isn't particularly crowded.

We find an even quieter dark corner where we can nurse our drinks in peace.

As she leans against the wall, her hair falls down her shoulders and a bit into her face.

I reach over and brush the loose strands away.

I can't fight the urge any longer.

I tilt her head back and press her lips to mine.

Her lips part softly and welcome me inside.

I let my tongue intertwine with hers as I press her against the wall.

I bury my fingers in her hair.

She pushes into me.

Her fingers run along my jawline and then down my neck.

When her hands reach my collarbone where my scars begin, I jolt away.

"I'm sorry," I mumble and pull myself together.

She stands before me hurt and dumbfounded.

"I'm sorry, I shouldn't have done that."

"No, you should have." She takes a step toward me and reaches for my face again.

But the moment is all wrong.

I step out of the shadows of the corner and my claustrophobia sets in again.

Everyone around me is laughing and talking.

I take a swig of the whiskey and finish the glass with a few gulps.

"I can't," I mumble and walk away from her.

CHAPTER 34 - JACKSON

WHEN I PULL AWAY...

The kiss was an impulse that I could no longer push away.

I wanted to do it since we first met.

I know it's wrong.

I know that I'm technically her boss and I should've kept my hands to myself.

But all of the years in isolation did not dull my senses that much.

I could tell that she wanted me, too, by the way her eyes scanned my body.

I caught her staring at my lips as I talked.

Sometimes, her tongue even ran across her lips as she looked at me.

That moment, in the dark corner, could've been perfect.

It was perfect briefly.

But then I ruined it.

Her hands drifted down my body and suddenly I remembered what was there.

I am sure that she could not feel my scars through my tuxedo, but her touch over them was enough to send me into a tailspin.

As soon as I step out of the comfort of that corner, I am exposed.

People start coming up to me and making introductions.

I am not an unfamiliar face among the rich and powerful of New York, but everyone is surprised to see me here in person.

I smile, shake hands, and exchange pleasantries.

The world is watching.

I cannot let anyone know how I feel inside.

I paint a plastic smile on my face and put up my guard.

I say charming things and quickly move from one couple to the next as people make their introductions.

When I've almost had enough, I excuse myself and head to the bar for another drink.

My thoughts come back to Harley over and over.

The feeling of suffocation and the

claustrophobia that I felt earlier in this mob seemed to have vanished and been replaced with only one thing; regret.

I scan the room to find her.

I don't see her at first.

I hope she did not leave.

I make my way around the perimeter of the room near the drapery that covers the walls of the ballroom.

On my second round, I see her talking to Phillips.

Phillips is about a head taller than Harley, dressed in a long strapless gown.

She is tall and elegant and so much more comfortable in heels than Harley.

"Oh, hey! Jackson!" Phillips gives me a warm hug as soon as I approach them. "I was just thanking Harley here for accompanying you out to this event."

Her voice is high and perky, just like it is on the phone.

She has worked for me since almost the beginning and hasn't changed much.

Even though she is now dressed in her evening wear, she frankly doesn't look much different than she does on the video conferencing calls we have.

I doubt that she ever met a Jimmy Choo heel that

she did not love; Phillips is impeccably put together at all times.

"She did me a big favor by coming," I say.

Harley nods, looking incredibly uncomfortable.

She wants to escape but clearly Phillips isn't letting her off that easily.

"I was just telling Harley that it's not every day that you make an appearance at one of these things. They can be incredibly dull."

"That would be the understatement of a lifetime," I say.

"Well, listen, let me go find Woodward so you can get this over with." Phillips leans over and gives Harley an unexpected hug and then practically prances away.

"I was going to leave, but she cornered me and wouldn't let me," Harley says. "But I'm going to go now."

She turns away from me and I reach for her. A jolt of electricity runs through me when we touch.

"No, please don't."

"I don't know what I did wrong."

"You did nothing wrong. It was all me. I am sorry."

I stare deeply into her eyes, but she looks away.

"I've wanted to kiss you for a very long time," I admit.

"You did?"

"Yes. More than anything."

A little smile forms at the corner of her lips.

"So, why did you...pull away?"

I look around.

"I can't tell you...here. But it was all my shit. Please don't leave."

She nods, not really believing me.

"I have to meet with this investor. And then we can go somewhere and...talk. My staff reserved a suite here upstairs just in case things got too much for me. We can go there and talk."

She shrugs her shoulders.

Before I can make a better case for my proposal, Phillips comes back with Woodward.

And makes the introduction.

WOODWARD IS a man in his late thirties with sprinkles of gray in his hair.

He is fit, the type to spend his spare time doing marathons and entering cycling competitions.

He has a strong handshake and is very good at pleasantries.

I reciprocate with equal charm.

When I introduce him to Harley, he lifts her hand up to his lips and kisses the back of it.

This throws her for a loop and she blushes and laughs.

"I've been watching your success, Mr. Ludlow," Woodward says.

"All of my friends call me Jackson. Please call me Jackson."

"In that case, I insist that you call me...Elliot," he says.

For a moment, I thought that he would make a terrible joke and ask me to call him Mr. Woodward, but he probably thought better of it.

If he had, then the conversation would come to a complete halt.

"You have built yourself quite an empire. It's very impressive."

"Thank you. And what about you? I am in awe of all of your accomplishments in solar."

I speak slowly because frankly I had forgotten what kind of business he was in and it just comes to me at the end.

"I appreciate you saying that," Woodward says.

"Well, I can see that you two are going to talk business, so I'm going to go get another drink," Harley says.

"I'm sorry to hear that," Woodward says. "It was a pleasure to meet you."

As she starts to walk away, I reach for her again. "Harley? I'll come find you after."

The only reason this needs saying is that I'm not sure if she is actually going to get a drink or is heading home.

She walks away without giving me an answer.

I want to go after her, but I can't be rude to Woodward.

So, I stand here and watch her walk away.

CHAPTER 35 - HARLEY

WHEN HE PULLS AWAY...

*H*e kisses me.

He walks up to me and presses his lips to mine.

He buries his hands in my hair and I run my fingers up the nape of his neck. His hands cradle my shoulders and our mouths intertwine.

This is the moment that I have been waiting for since we met, and yet it takes me completely by surprise.

And then, just like that, it is over.

He just pulls away from me and walks away.

Why?

Did I do something wrong?

Did my breath smell bad?

Did he think that he'd made a mistake?

Probably.

It is difficult to describe the embarrassment I feel in that moment.

One moment we are connected more than we ever were before, expressing our feelings for each other in this passionate physical act, and the next, he just leaves.

Tears start to well up in my eyes, and I walk out of the shadows to make them go away.

I don't dare follow him.

I go in the opposite direction toward the exit.

He clearly doesn't need me here.

Not that I would stay anyway.

The rejection is just too much to deal with.

But then a tall, flamingo of a woman comes up to me and refuses to leave me alone.

She works for Jackson and knows all about me.

"Thank you so much for coming here with him. I am not sure if he would've otherwise," she says in her annoying happy voice.

Can't she see that I'm in pain?

That I don't want to talk to her.

She either doesn't or she does and doesn't give a shit.

"I'm actually on my way to get another drink," I say, trying to escape.

"Perfect. I'll come with you."

As she follows me to the bar where I had no intentions of going, she continues to talk about Jackson.

How difficult of a time he has had over the last few years and how important this investor is to their company.

I get the sense that she has been with Jackson for a long time.

After the bartender hands me my drink, I take a few sips and feel a little better.

As Avery Phillips talks, I decide that I did nothing wrong and I shouldn't be embarrassed about anything.

Suddenly, whatever shame I'd felt earlier morphs into anger and rage.

I am here supporting him, and he treats me like that?

First, he kisses me out of the blue and then he rejects me?

Well, who the hell does he think he is?

I don't need to be treated like this.

"So, I know a little bit about how you two met. I'm really sorry that happened to you," Avery says after noticing that I haven't said anything in a while.

"Perfect." I shake my head.

"Oh, I'm sorry, I really shouldn't have brought it up."

"No, it's fine. I'm just not in the best mood right now. Actually, I have a headache. I think I'm going to go home."

She nods compassionately, but I can tell by the expression on her face that my decision is unacceptable to her.

And then Jackson shows up.

She wraps her arms around him, giving him a warm and almost passionate embrace.

As I stand here watching them, it finally hits me.

I'm such a fool.

Of course.

Avery wants him.

She has been working for him for ages and has had feelings for him all along.

Why wouldn't she?

He looks perfect, at least on the outside.

Well, she can have him.

Whatever feelings I had for him have evaporated and have been replaced with anger and disappointment.

I thought that he was different from the other men I'd met, but he isn't.

He is just more fucked up in the head than the others and his games are more complicated.

When Avery finally leaves to find this Woodward guy, I walk away but Jackson grabs my hand.

"Please don't."

I want to just walk away and never see him again, but my anger gets the best of me.

And I demand an answer.

"I don't know what I did wrong."

"You did nothing wrong. It was all me. I am sorry."

I glare at him, but his eyes put me in a trance and I look away.

"I've wanted to kiss you for a very long time," he says.

His voice is soft and tender and apologetic.

It comes out of the blue and takes me by surprise.

I don't want to believe him, but for some reason I do.

"You did?"

"Yes. More than anything."

Don't be such a chump, Harley.

He's just playing a game.

"So, why did you...pull away?"

He doesn't have a good answer.

226

He can't tell me here, whatever the fuck that means.

"Please don't leave," he pleads.

If I were to stay I need a better answer than that, but our conversation is interrupted by Avery and Elliot Woodward who takes me by surprise and actually kisses the back of my hand when he meets me.

He is charming and disarming, saying exactly the right thing at the right moment.

What surprises me even more is how well Jackson matches each one of Elliot's charming comments with his own.

It's like they are playing a game of tennis with two people of equal skill.

The ball keeps going back and forth between the players without scoring one point.

It's hard to believe that this is Jackson after years of isolation.

He doesn't miss a step or an opportunity to both flatter Elliot and to showcase his own success.

When there's a brief pause, I see my way out and excuse myself.

Jackson is distracted and he can't follow me, so this is the best time to leave.

But right before I go, he again asks me to stay.

I walk away without giving him an answer.

I look around for Avery and see that she is laughing and mingling with a large group of equally gorgeous women a few tables away.

This is my chance.

I walk briskly toward the double doors and into the lobby.

I ask the bellboy to call me a cab.

As I wait, I start to feel anxious about getting into a car with a stranger again.

"Your car is ready, ma'am."

CHAPTER 36 - HARLEY

WHEN I LEAVE...

When the car arrives, I don't get in.

I can't.

I try, but I stand here frozen in the lobby.

"I'm sorry, I've changed my mind."

"Perfectly alright, ma'am," the bellboy says without a tinge of surprise.

I feel like I have to explain; I'm relieved that he walks away before I can come up with a good reason.

There is no good reason.

I just can't make myself get into a car with a strange man I don't know.

I step outside and look for the SUV which we arrived in.

Would it be inappropriate if I asked Mr. Garbo to drive me home?

I can even pay him for the ride.

Unfortunately, he is nowhere to be found.

A gust of wind swirls past me, shivering, I head back inside.

"Would you like me to call you another cab?" The bellboy walks up to me.

I thought that he was distracted with someone else, but he is a bit too attentive to his guests.

"No, I'm fine. I'm sorry, I was just...looking for someone."

"Of course," he says and leaves me alone.

I walk back inside the lobby and think about my options.

If I don't want to call a ride-share company then my only other choice is to take the subway.

I look down at my beautiful gown.

It's tailored so that my heels are only slightly visible, which is fine for walking around a hotel lobby and the party.

But if I were to take this dress on the subway, it's for sure going to get ruined from the filth and dirt.

Also, these shoes aren't exactly made for walking down blocks, at least not by the inexpert heel walker like I am.

No, I can't take the subway.

My toes will freeze and fall off walking the few

blocks to it and then from the subway to my place and I will ruin the shoes and the dress, something I can't really afford to do.

I go to the bathroom to collect my thoughts. I need to gather the strength to get into a cab.

After using the bathroom, I wash my hands and look at my reflection in the mirror.

I watched a YouTube video, borrowed Julie's contouring kit to achieve the look, and I'm quite pleased with how it turned out.

I give myself a reassuring smile.

Everything is going to be okay.

I just need to take a deep breath and get into the cab.

Nothing bad is going to happen.

Parker doesn't know where I am.

I'm safe.

But the sad eyes of the girl looking back at me aren't convinced.

I take my time heading back into the lobby.

I don't want to ask for another cab again just in case I can't summon the strength to get into it.

"Harley, wait!" I know by his smooth silky voice who it is without even turning around.

A part of me is relieved that he is here to stop me from getting into a cab with a stranger.

"What do you want, Jackson?"

"Can we talk?"

"Fine, talk."

"In private."

I look around the place.

There are a few people around but no one right next to us. "There's no one here."

He shakes his head. "I can't tell you this here. I have a suite upstairs. There's food there. I will tell you everything there."

"I need Mr. Garbo to drive me home," I say definitively.

"He will, anytime you want."

"I want to go now."

He pulls out his phone.

"What are you doing?"

"Messaging him." He types on the screen. "He will be here in five minutes."

He takes a step back from me.

His face is severe and without much expression.

"Thank you."

"I'm sorry if I hurt you," he says. "I shouldn't have kissed you."

Is that what he thinks?

Then he's a bigger idiot than I thought.

"Yes, you should've kissed me. You shouldn't

have just pulled away and left without an explanation."

He takes a deep breath, as if he's gathering his thoughts.

"What? What is such a big deal?" I demand to know.

He reaches for his tie, but instead of adjusting its perfect knot, he loosens it around his neck.

Then he unbuttons the top button.

And the one below it.

I furrow my brows.

"What are you doing?"

Without another word, he puts his finger in the air, indicating for me to wait.

Another button is freed.

He pulls his tie to the side and pulls down on his shirt.

I lean over.

His beautiful soft olive skin comes to an abrupt and jagged end right under his collarbone.

Below that is all scar tissue.

The wounds have healed a long time ago, but the scars have remained as a horrific reminder of the past.

I reach out and flinch when I touch it.

The thought of what could've caused these sends shivers through me.

We stand locked in silence for a few moments.

He watches me look at his scars with a glazed expression on his face.

His eyes are like ice.

When I am finished, he buttons his shirt back up again.

"I pulled away because your hand ran over them. I knew you couldn't feel them through my tux, but I wasn't ready for *that*."

"I'm...sorry," I whisper.

With a few expert movements, he fixes his tie. His phone goes off.

"Mr. Garbo is here. Have a good night."

CHAPTER 37 - JACKSON

WHILE I WAIT...

I need to make her understand what happened.

Just telling her about the scars isn't going to be enough.

And if she doesn't want me then, well, that's it.

I stand before her as the lobby slowly fills up with people and loosen my tie.

I unbutton one button.

And then the next.

The shirt opens wide enough for her to see. She lets out a little gasp as she looks.

My phone vibrates in my pocket.

I tell her that her driver is here.

I turn on my heels and walk away from her. I feel

her gaze burning on my back, but I don't pause or change the speed of my pace.

She is free to go and whatever she decides to do now is up to her.

I head straight up to the suite that my assistant arranged for me on the nineteenth floor.

It is a two bedroom penthouse with spectacular views from each floor-to-ceiling window and the terrace.

I pour myself another glass of whiskey and take my drink outside.

After all of that time with people, it's nice to be alone again.

Out here, high above the city, I can hear myself think.

The room's phone goes off, intruding on my privacy.

I pick it up.

"I'm sorry to bother you, sir, but there's a young lady here to see you. Harley Burke."

I smile. "Send her up."

Harley rings the doorbell a few minutes later.

"Thanks for coming," I say, leaning on the door after I open it. I'm no longer wearing the jacket of my tuxedo and I've taken off my tie.

"Thanks for inviting me," she says shyly.

Her hair falls slightly in her face and it takes all of my strength not to brush it away.

But I don't want to push things.

I'm glad she's here and that's enough for now.

I lick my lips and give her a small smile.

"Do you want a drink?"

"Yes. Of water, please."

"Not drinking anymore?"

"I've had my fill. I already have a headache."

"You're a lightweight."

She shrugs and walks in the living room.

After looking around at the modern furniture and the gigantic paintings on the walls, Harley plops down on the white linen sofa in the corner and starts to unbuckle her shoes.

"I'm sorry to be so informal, but I have to take these things off. They are awful."

"I didn't know there were women who didn't like Jimmy Choo," I joke.

She shrugs. "They may be pretty, but comfortable they are not. At least, not to me. I don't know, maybe if I were more like Avery then that's all I would wear."

I narrow my eyes.

What is she getting at?

I hand her a glass of water.

"Listen, just because I took off my shoes doesn't mean that I'm staying," she says, downing a few big gulps.

"Noted."

I lean casually on the kitchen island and wait for her to tell me what's on her mind.

"So...what's with your scars?"

I swirl the whiskey around the bottom of my glass and admire how the amber liquid dances in the light.

"There isn't much to tell. There was an accident. I got burned."

"It sounds like there should be more to the story than that," she presses me.

I shrug. "Not tonight."

I've given her an explanation for pulling away from her, but that doesn't mean that I'm ready to give her more.

"It has been a really long day," I add.

She nods and stands up onto her tiptoes and then brings herself down again.

In her bare feet, her gown reaches way past her feet and, for a moment, she looks like a little girl wearing her mother's dress.

"Okay, fine, you don't have to tell me about that. I understand that it's difficult to talk about, but what about Avery?"

Avery?

"Oh, you mean Phillips? What about her?" I ask. What on earth is causing her to bring her up?

"Did you ever date her?"

"No."

"Sleep with her?"

"No."

"Did you ever want to?"

"No."

"You're such a liar," she says, rolling her eyes.

"Phillips is my colleague. She works with me."

"I work with you."

"Okay...maybe that's not the best explanation," I say.

"I just don't get it. She's gorgeous and so...perfect. Seems like she would be more your type."

I take a step closer to her.

And then another. I look straight into her eyes.

"Well, she's not," I say sternly. "I never liked her like that. And she never liked me like that."

"Now, that I totally don't believe," she says, shaking her head. "I mean, I saw the way she was looking at you all night. She is really into you."

I take another step forward.

We are so close that I can feel her breath on my body.

I lift up her chin and look deep into her eyes.

"I'm sorry, I don't mean to be so...jealous or insecure. It's just that I saw the way that she looked at you and you at her. And you have such a long history."

"Harley," I say, pressing my lips onto hers. "There is nothing going on between Avery and me. And trust me, if there was, then I'd have someone a lot scarier to answer to."

She pulls away from me with a perplexed expression on her face.

"Her wife," I explain and kiss her again.

"Avery is married to a woman?" she asks, pulling away again.

I nod and kiss her again.

As our lips touch, hers part and welcome me inside.

CHAPTER 38 - HARLEY

WHEN I STAY...

He takes me into his arms and presses his lips onto mine.

He groans and tilts his head, sealing his mouth over mine. His lips feel soft and firm at the same time.

There's a gentleness to the pressure he exerts that gives me butterflies in the pit of my stomach.

His fingers run up my spine and pull lightly at my hair at the bottom of my neck.

But as our kiss gets more passionate, they quickly bury themselves, deeper and deeper.

His tongue dips inside of me for a moment as if he is tasting me.

Then his lips part and I breathe out a sigh.

My fingers make their way up his jawline and toward his face.

Then I run them down his back, squeezing softly.

My hands are in his hair.

He moans a little, and it sounds a lot like a growl.

Our kiss deepens as we get more comfortable with each other.

Suddenly, it's as if our mouths are devouring each other's.

Pressing so hard into his body, I feel his heart beating against me.

His body is giving off so much heat that I get drenched in sweat.

Cupping the small of my back with one hand and my buttocks with another, he easily lifts me up into the air and carries me to the bedroom.

I have thought about this moment for a very long time.

The moment that I would not be virginal anymore.

How would it go?

Something like this.

I would date a guy for a few weeks, maybe a month. I would take my time getting ready for the big night.

I would admit my secret to him and he would take a few days to think about it.

Being someone's first in her twenties is different than being her first as a teenager.

Back then, most people are virgins so you're not this unusual, awkward, sad creature that someone has to take pity on.

This process wasn't really a fantasy but the reality that I had braced myself for.

Nowhere in this reality did I imagine that my first time would be filled with passion and lust and everything that people only have in books.

That's not real life, right?

Except that it is.

When Jackson brings me to the bedroom, he stands me up on my feet and brushes my hair to the front.

Then he reaches for the zipper and lets my gown fall to the floor.

With another swift motion, he pushes me onto the bed and presses his body on top of mine.

I ache for him.

When he tries to move his lips down my body, I bring his head back up to mine and kiss him again and again.

"Stay," he says firmly and slowly starts to make his way down my body.

As his lips touch my shoulders and then head toward my breasts, I realize how heavy they've become.

Tender even, aroused.

He pulls off my bra and takes his time with each, giving each part of them equal attention.

I lose myself in the moment and then come back with an incessant need for more.

This isn't enough.

My body throbs for his and I need him inside of me now.

Continuing to kiss me, he takes off his tie and I reach for his shirt. But he pushes my arms away.

"C'mon, please."

"No. Tonight we are going to do something different."

My heart skips a beat.

Different?

I haven't even done the regular thing.

"Do you trust me?" he asks.

I look into his eyes and I know that I'm in good hands. I give him a nod.

"Scoot up a little to the head of the bed," he says. I do as he says.

Then he takes the tie and wraps it around the loop in the middle of the headboard.

My heartbeat doubles in intensity with each one of my breaths as he raises my hands above my head and ties them to the headboard.

"Do you like this?" he asks, taking my breast in his mouth.

I clench my legs from anticipation.

"But I can't touch you."

"That's okay. You won't be able to see me either."

"What?"

He glides off the bed and walks over to the closet.

He takes another tie from a hanger and sits down next to me.

"Do you want this?" he whispers into my ear, running the tie in between my legs.

"But then I won't be able to see you."

"Then you'll feel even more."

I inhale deeply and slowly, trying to calm myself down.

I should be freaking out.

But I'm not.

This feels so...right.

He moves his fingers along my hipbones and then lets them linger on top of my panties.

He's toying with me.

Arousing me.

And it's working.

"Tell me you want this," he says, dangling the other tie in front of me.

"Yes," I moan, my whole body begging him to come inside of me.

"Tell me you want this," he says, running the tie in between my breasts.

"I want this."

After the blindfold is secure, he lifts my right leg and starts kissing around the inside of my ankle, slowly inching his way up.

When I cinch my legs closed unable to handle all the pleasure, he opens them up again.

"I want you," I say. "I need you...inside of me."

"That's quite a demanding request from someone who is blindfolded and tied up."

"Please," I beg.

With one swift motion, he pulls off my underwear.

I hear the clinking of a belt and the sound of his pants falling to the floor.

The sound of something rubber being put on.

A moment later, he opens my legs.

He runs his fingers over me and then pushes them deep inside.

I moan and he swirls them around and says, "You are so tight."

My breathing speeds up and I feel the rise and fall of my chest, even though I can't see it.

Suddenly, with his fingers massaging me, I feel a sudden run of warmth spring out from somewhere inside of me.

"Come for me," he whispers and speeds up his movements.

My whole body starts to shake. I clench my legs together and let the wave come over me. A moment later, my body goes limp.

"That was...amazing," I mumble, slurring my speech.

"Oh, we're not done yet," he says, sending a shock of electricity through me with his words.

When he opens my legs up again, my body immediately strains and yearns for him.

Slowly, he pushes himself inside of me.

This time his hands are holding onto mine and his lips are kissing mine.

I wrap my legs around his butt and push him deeper inside of me.

This is what I've been craving ever since I first saw him.

"You are so tight," he groans.

At first his thrusts are slow, but they quickly speed up just like his kisses.

As they build momentum, our movements border on violence, but a good kind of violence.

Warmth again starts to build up somewhere inside of me.

This time, however, the feeling is familiar and it doesn't catch me off-guard.

"Oh, Harley," Jackson moans into my ear, saying each syllable of my name as if they are separate words.

His thrusts slow down and he slowly relaxes his body on top of me.

It is only then when his chest lays on top of mine that I feel the roughness of his scars against my soft skin.

CHAPTER 39 - HARLEY

AFTERWARD...

We fall asleep in each other's arms soon after.

Our bodies intertwine and neither of us know where one begins and the other one ends.

It's dawn when I finally rouse.

I open my eyes slowly and look at the man lying asleep next to me.

His breathing is steady and strong, and I can hear his heartbeat in his chest.

My eyes run over his luscious lips, full of life, not chapped like mine after a night of lovemaking, and down his body.

Right below his collarbone is where the scar tissue begins.

Thick and uneven, it covers his body to his belly button.

Cuts with a knife are sharp.

A bullet from a gunshot is similarly localized.

No, these scars were caused by something particularly unforgiving, fire.

My hand recoils a little as my fingers run over the scar tissue, not because the burns repulse me but because of the pain that I imagine he must've felt.

I don't even let my mind go there.

"Hey…" Jackson says, slowly opening his eyes. "Good morning."

I prop myself up on my elbow and kiss him on the lips.

"Thank you for last night," I say.

He smiles and pulls me closer to him.

"Thank you." His voice is low and strained, still half asleep. "You ready for more?"

I would be lying if I said that the thought hadn't crossed my mind, so it takes considerable strength to pull away from him.

"I have to tell you something first."

I take a deep breath as he waits.

Maybe I shouldn't say it.

I doubt that he knows.

I consider this for a moment.

"I'm a virgin."

"No, you're not." He laughs.

"No, I mean, I'm not now. But I was...before."

He sits up and leans his head against the headboard.

His arm muscles bulge with each movement and I can't help but lick my lips looking at them.

"Why didn't you tell me this before?"

I shrug.

There are so many reasons.

I just didn't want him to reject me.

I didn't want him to think I was...odd.

I didn't want our first time to be tainted by this inadequacy.

But mainly, I didn't tell him because I didn't want to talk about it.

I didn't want to think about it anymore than I already have.

"I was just so...into what we were doing," I say after a moment. "I just wanted to keep going. I didn't want to stop."

He smiles.

"Did you enjoy it?"

"Yes, a million times yes."

"Good. Well, you're a natural."

. . .

* * *

The conversation goes a lot smoother than I had imagined it would.

Jackson hardly seems phased by what I have revealed at all and I'm glad for that.

Since neither of us ate much at last night's party, we are both famished and order room service.

"So, how did it go with Elliot last night?" I ask, digging into my omelette when the food arrives.

"Actually, quite well. We seem to have a lot in common and he seemed to be really interested in Minetta."

"That's great."

He nods, eating a bite of his bagel with cream cheese and lox.

"He's having a winter party at his house in the Hamptons and he invited us."

"Us?"

He shrugs.

"Yes, both of us. I guess he only invited me, and I could take another girl if you'd prefer that, though."

"Shut up." I laugh. "What kind of party is it?"

"It's a masquerade ball. Costumes. Masks. The whole nine yards."

"Wow, that's...intense."

"Tell me about it."

Then it hits me.

"I'm sorry, I should've asked you earlier. But how are you feeling about everything? Being out in public and all?"

"Um...it's an adjustment, for sure. But, it's actually not as bad as I thought it was going to be."

"Are you sure you're not just saying that?"

"Well, I didn't have a panic attack yet." He smiles. "Either way, I don't really have a choice when it comes to going to this party. Woodward needs to see me as someone he can socialize with; that's the only way he'll invest. And if I don't want to have layoffs then I need his investment."

He could've easily been one of those CEOs who doesn't care about his employees, but he isn't.

He is making a sacrifice to save their jobs.

I really admire that. I lean over and give him a kiss.

AFTERWARD...

She is lying in my arms.

Her fingers are running down my scars and she isn't repulsed.

I have not let myself get close to another woman in years.

It was actually one of the things that drove me to hide myself away from humanity. I met her at a bar.

I was feeling lonely and she was, too.

She was pretty enough for a night of comfort.

She also seemed nice.

I thought that when she saw me, she would offer me an ounce of kindness.

Unfortunately, she did not.

As soon as I took off my shirt, her face became

contorted in repulsion. Then, she quickly made an excuse and left.

Her expression said everything that I feared I was now.

A monster.

Un-human.

Someone no one would ever want to see, let alone be with again.

And now, Harley came into my life.

Crashed into it, is more like it.

I stroke her hair and lose myself in the moment.

I haven't felt so...at peace, in a very long time.

A part of me feels guilty, of course.

How dare I move on with my life after what happened?

How dare I let a little bit of beauty and love back into it?

But I tried putting that part of me into a dark corner and never letting it out. I tried dwelling on my grief.

None of those things made the grief anymore bearable.

None of those things brought anyone back from the dead.

They just made my life feel a lot like death.

I lived.

I worked.

I hardly mattered.

And now?

Well, now I have Harley.

That's...something.

Suddenly, I have something to look forward to again.

It's like my life has been night for almost four years.

And now, out of the blue, the sun is starting to peek over the horizon.

In the dark, you make your way around the only way you know how.

You feel your way.

You memorize your steps.

You take the same path back and forth, and quickly the days disappear into a monotonous cycle.

But then the sun comes, with its rays of light, you open your eyes and really start to look.

Oh, so that's what this world actually looks like.

Perhaps it's not as gloomy as I thought it was.

At least now, I have light.

When Harley asks me about Woodward and I tell her about the masquerade party, I actually have something resembling excitement running through me.

It's a public event that I have to attend, but it's not one that I have to necessarily dread.

Before, when things like this came up, I always tried to go but eventually gave up on trying and just resorted to my usual list of explanations for why I couldn't.

But now...the thought of going to a winter wonderland party is actually enticing.

What's going to happen there?

Who's going to be there?

What's it going to look like?

And most importantly, what will Harley look like and how soon after the party can I undress her?

"I have to check my phone. I'm sure that Julie is freaking out that I haven't texted her," Harley says.

I nod, sitting up and leaning against the headboard.

The tie that I used to blindfold her is still lying next to me on the pillow.

Looking at it gives me a thrill and I feel my whole body get tense just thinking about what we just did.

As soon as she puts down her phone, I'm going to pull her on top of me.

This time she will be on top.

This time she will be the one looking down at me.

"Wow, I have five missed calls and three voice messages. That's weird. Julie hates leaving voice messages."

She stands next to the nightstand, wrapped in a sheet.

"Oh my God," Harley whispers, putting her hand over her mouth as she listens.

"What's wrong?"

"My mother's in the hospital. She had an accident."

She sits down on the edge of the bed and frantically dials a phone number.

"Dad, what happened?"

She is close enough to me that I can hear every word clearly.

"She was hit by a car, honey," a tired voice on the other end says. "You need to come here as soon as possible."

As they talk, her whole body trembles.

I wrap my arms around her shoulders and try to keep her warm.

Her father is a man of few words and everything comes out as a fragment of a complete thought.

"Okay, Dad, let me figure some things out and then I'll call you back."

Harley hangs up the phone and buries her head in my chest.

I hold her until she pulls away.

"I'm sorry," she says over and over again. "I don't know why I'm crying so much. I'm such a mess."

"Your mother is gravely injured. It's perfectly normal to cry."

She shakes her head and sobs. "No, it's not that. I mean, it is, but it's not that entirely."

"What is it, Harley?" I ask, looking deep into her eyes.

"The thing is that I can't do it."

I don't understand what she means. I look at her and wait for an explanation.

"I *can't* go home."

THANK you for reading Tangled up in Ice!

I hope you enjoyed Harley and Jackson's story. Can't wait to find out what happens next?

One-click Tangled up in Pain now!

Everything comes at a price. What if this one is too high even for him to pay?

Jackson Ludlow, the recluse billionaire of New

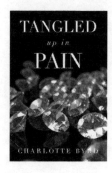

York, is beautiful and captivating but also damaged and alone.

He thinks he is the only one with secrets, but he's wrong.

My past is coming for me. It's forcing me back there: the place that ruined everything.

I don't want to go. He can't make me.

But there's no way out.

One-click Tangled up in Pain now!

Sign up for my **newsletter** to find out when I have new books!

You can also join my Facebook group, **Charlotte Byrd's Reader Club**, for exclusive giveaways and sneak peaks of future books.

I appreciate you sharing my books and telling your friends about them. Reviews help readers find my books! Please leave a review on your favorite site.

Want to read a "Decadent, delicious, & dangerously addictive!" romance you will not be able to put down? The entire series is out! 1-Click Black Edge NOW!

I don't belong here.

I'm in way over my head. But I have debts to pay.

They call my name. The spotlight is on. The auction starts.

Mr. Black is the highest bidder. He's dark, rich, and powerful. He likes to play games.

The only rule is there are no rules.

But it's just one night. **What's the worst that can happen?**

1-Click BLACK EDGE Now!

* * *

START READING BLACK EDGE ON THE NEXT PAGE!

CHAPTER 1- ELLIE

WHEN THE INVITATION ARRIVES...

"Here it is! Here it is!" my roommate Caroline yells at the top of her lungs as she runs into my room.

We were friends all through Yale and we moved to New York together after graduation.

Even though I've known Caroline for what feels like a million years, I am still shocked by the exuberance of her voice. It's quite loud given the smallness of her body.

Caroline is one of those super skinny girls who can eat pretty much anything without gaining a pound.

Unfortunately, I am not that talented. In fact, my body seems to have the opposite gift. I can eat nothing but vegetables for a week straight, eat one slice of pizza, and gain a pound.

"What is it?" I ask, forcing myself to sit up.

It's noon and I'm still in bed.

My mother thinks I'm depressed and wants me to see her shrink.

She might be right, but I can't fathom the strength.

"The invitation!" Caroline says jumping in bed next to me.

I stare at her blankly.

And then suddenly it hits me.

This must be *the* invitation.

"You mean...it's..."

"Yes!" she screams and hugs me with excitement.

"Oh my God!" She gasps for air and pulls away from me almost as quickly.

"Hey, you know I didn't brush my teeth yet," I say turning my face away from hers.

"Well, what are you waiting for? Go brush them," she instructs.

Begrudgingly, I make my way to the bathroom.

We have been waiting for this invitation for some time now.

And by we, I mean Caroline.

I've just been playing along, pretending to care, not really expecting it to show up.

Without being able to contain her excitement, Caroline bursts through the door when my mouth is still full of toothpaste.

She's jumping up and down, holding a box in her hand.

"Wait, what's that?" I mumble and wash my mouth out with water.

"This is it!" Caroline screeches and pulls me into the living room before I have a chance to wipe my mouth with a towel.

"But it's a box," I say staring at her.

"Okay, okay," Caroline takes a couple of deep yoga breaths, exhaling loudly.

She puts the box carefully on our dining room table. There's no address on it.

It looks something like a fancy gift box with a big monogrammed C in the middle.

Is the C for Caroline?

"Is this how it came? There's no address on it?" I ask.

"It was hand-delivered," Caroline whispers.

I hold my breath as she carefully removes the top part, revealing the satin and silk covered wood box inside.

The top of it is gold plated with whimsical twirls all around the edges, and the mirrored area is engraved with her full name.

Caroline Elizabeth Kennedy Spruce.

Underneath her name is a date, one week in the future. 8 PM.

We stare at it for a few moments until Caroline reaches for the elegant knob to open the box.

Inside, Caroline finds a custom monogram made of foil in gold on silk emblazoned on the inside of the flap cover.

There's also a folio covered in silk. Caroline carefully opens the folio and finds another foil monogram and the invitation.

The inside invitation is one layer, shimmer white, with gold writing.

"Is this for real? How many layers of invitation are there?" I ask.

But the presentation is definitely doing its job. We are both duly impressed.

"There's another knob," I say, pointing to the knob in front of the box.

I'm not sure how we had missed it before.

Caroline carefully pulls on this knob, revealing a drawer that holds the inserts (a card with directions and a response card).

"Oh my God, I can't go to this alone," Caroline mumbles, turning to me.

I stare blankly at her.

Getting invited to this party has been her dream ever since she found out about it from someone in the Cicada 17, a super-secret society at Yale.

"Look, here, it says that I can bring a friend," she yells out even though I'm standing right next to her.

"It probably says a date. A plus one?" I say.

"No, a friend. Girl preferred," Caroline reads off the invitation card.

That part of the invitation is in very small ink, as if someone made the person stick it on, without their express permission.

"I don't want to crash," I say.

Frankly, I don't really want to go.

These kind of upper-class events always make me feel a little bit uncomfortable.

"Hey, aren't you supposed to be at work?" I ask.

"Eh, I took a day off," Caroline says waving her arm. "I knew that the invitation would come today and I just couldn't deal with work. You know how it is."

I nod. Sort of.

Caroline and I seem like we come from the same world.

We both graduated from private school, we both went to Yale, and our parents belong to the same exclusive country club in Greenwich, Connecticut.

But we're not really that alike.

Caroline's family has had money for many generations going back to the railroads.

My parents were an average middle class family from Connecticut.

They were both teachers and our idea of summering was renting a 1-bedroom bungalow near Clearwater, FL for a week.

But then my parents got divorced when I was 8, and my mother started tutoring kids to make extra money.

The pay was the best in Greenwich, where parents paid more than $100 an hour.

And that's how she met, Mitch Willoughby, my stepfather.

He was a widower with a five-year old daughter who was not doing well after her mom's untimely death.

Even though Mom didn't usually tutor anyone younger than 12, she agreed to take a meeting with Mitch and his daughter because $200 an hour was too much to turn down.

Three months later, they were in love and six

months later, he asked her to marry him on top of the Eiffel Tower.

They got married, when I was 11, in a huge 450-person ceremony in Nantucket.

So even though Caroline and I run in the same circles, we're not really from the same circle.

It has nothing to do with her, she's totally accepting, it's me.

I don't always feel like I belong.

Caroline majored in art-history at Yale, and she now works at an exclusive contemporary art gallery in Soho.

It's chic and tiny, featuring only 3 pieces of art at a time.

Ash, the owner - I'm not sure if that's her first or last name - mainly keeps the space as a showcase. What the gallery really specializes in is going to wealthy people's homes and choosing their art for them.

They're basically interior designers, but only for art.

None of the pieces sell for anything less than $200 grand, but Caroline's take home salary is about $21,000.

Clearly, not enough to pay for our 2 bedroom apartment in Chelsea.

Her parents cover her part of the rent and pay all of her other expenses.

Mine do too, of course.

Well, Mitch does.

I only make about $27,000 at my writer's assistant job and that's obviously not covering my half of our $6,000 per month apartment.

So, what's the difference between me and Caroline?

I guess the only difference is that I feel bad about taking the money.

I have a $150,000 school loan from Yale that I don't want Mitch to pay for.

It's my loan and I'm going to pay for it myself, dammit.

Plus, unlike Caroline, I know that real people don't really live like this.

Real people like my dad, who is being pressured to sell the house for more than a million dollars that he and my mom bought back in the late 80's (the neighborhood has gone up in price and teachers now have to make way for tech entrepreneurs and real estate moguls).

"How can you just not go to work like that? Didn't you use all of your sick days flying to Costa Rica last month?" I ask.

"Eh, who cares? Ash totally understands. Besides, she totally owes me. If it weren't for me, she would've never closed that geek millionaire who had the hots for me and ended up buying close to a million dollars' worth of art for his new mansion."

Caroline does have a way with men.

She's fun and outgoing and perky.

The trick, she once told me, is to figure out exactly what the guy wants to hear.

Because a geek millionaire, as she calls anyone who has made money in tech, does not want to hear the same thing that a football player wants to hear.

And neither of them want to hear what a trust fund playboy wants to hear.

But Caroline isn't a gold digger.

Not at all.

Her family owns half the East Coast.

And when it comes to men, she just likes to have fun.

I look at the time.

It's my day off, but that doesn't mean that I want to spend it in bed in my pajamas, listening to Caroline obsessing over what she's going to wear.

No, today, is my day to actually get some writing done.

I'm going to Starbucks, getting a table in the

back, near the bathroom, and am actually going to finish this short story that I've been working on for a month.

Or maybe start a new one.

I go to my room and start getting dressed.

I have to wear something comfortable, but something that's not exactly work clothes.

I hate how all of my clothes have suddenly become work clothes. It's like they've been tainted.

They remind me of work and I can't wear them out anymore on any other occasion. I'm not a big fan of my work, if you can't tell.

Caroline follows me into my room and plops down on my bed.

I take off my pajamas and pull on a pair of leggings.

Ever since these have become the trend, I find myself struggling to force myself into a pair of jeans.

They're just so comfortable!

"Okay, I've come to a decision," Caroline says. "You *have* to come with me!"

"Oh, I have to come with you?" I ask, incredulously. "Yeah, no, I don't think so."

"Oh c'mon! Please! Pretty please! It will be so much fun!"

"Actually, you can't make any of those promises.

You have no idea what it will be," I say, putting on a long sleeve shirt and a sweater with a zipper in the front.

Layers are important during this time of year.

The leaves are changing colors, winds are picking up, and you never know if it's going to be one of those gorgeous warm, crisp New York days they like to feature in all those romantic comedies or a soggy, overcast dreary day that only shows up in one scene at the end when the two main characters fight or break up (but before they get back together again).

"Okay, yes, I see your point," Caroline says, sitting up and crossing her legs. "But here is what we *do* know. We do know that it's going to be amazing. I mean, look at the invitation. It's a freakin' box with engravings and everything!"

Usually, Caroline is much more eloquent and better at expressing herself.

"Okay, yes, the invitation is impressive," I admit.

"And as you know, the invitation is everything. I mean, it really sets the mood for the party. The event! And not just the mood. It establishes a certain expectation. And this box..."

"Yes, the invitation definitely sets up a certain expectation," I agree.

"So?"

"So?" I ask her back.

"Don't you want to find out what that expectation is?"

"No." I shake my head categorically.

"Okay. So what else do we know?" Caroline asks rhetorically as I pack away my Mac into my bag.

"I have to go, Caroline," I say.

"No, listen. The yacht. Of course, the yacht. How could I bury the lead like that?" She jumps up and down with excitement again.

"We also know that it's going to be this super exclusive event on a *yacht*! And not just some small 100 footer, but a *mega*-yacht."

I stare at her blankly, pretending to not be impressed.

When Caroline first found out about this party, through her ex-boyfriend, we spent days trying to figure out what made this event so special.

But given that neither of us have been on a yacht before, at least not a mega-yacht – we couldn't quite get it.

"You know the yacht is going to be amazing!"

"Yes, of course," I give in. "But that's why I'm sure that you're going to have a wonderful time by yourself. I have to go."

I grab my keys and toss them into the bag.

"Ellie," Caroline says.

The tone of her voice suddenly gets very serious, to match the grave expression on her face.

"Ellie, please. I don't think I can go by myself."

CHAPTER 2 - ELLIE

WHEN YOU HAVE COFFEE WITH A GUY YOU CAN'T HAVE...

*A*nd that's pretty much how I was roped into going.

You don't know Caroline, but if you did, the first thing you'd find out is that she is not one to take things seriously.

Nothing fazes her.

Nothing worries her.

Sometimes she is the most enlightened person on earth, other times she's the densest.

Most of the time, I'm jealous of the fact that she simply lives life in the present.

"So, you're going?" my friend Tom asks.

He brought me my pumpkin spice latte, the first one of the season!

I close my eyes and inhale it's sweet aroma before taking the first sip.

But even before its wonderful taste of cinnamon and nutmeg runs down my throat, Tom is already criticizing my decision.

"I can't believe you're actually going," he says.

"Oh my God, now I know it's officially fall," I change the subject.

"Was there actually such a thing as autumn before the pumpkin spice latte? I mean, I remember that we had falling leaves, changing colors, all that jazz, but without this...it's like Christmas without a Christmas tree."

"Ellie, it's a day after Labor Day," Tom rolls his eyes. "It's not fall yet."

I take another sip. "Oh yes, I do believe it is."

"Stop changing the subject," Tom takes a sip of his plain black coffee.

How he doesn't get bored with that thing, I'll never know.

But that's the thing about Tom.

He's reliable.

Always on time, never late.

It's nice. That's what I have always liked about him.

He's basically the opposite of Caroline in every way.

And that's what makes seeing him like this, as only a friend, so hard.

"Why are you going there? Can't Caroline go by herself?" Tom asks, looking straight into my eyes.

His hair has this annoying tendency of falling into his face just as he's making a point – as a way of accentuating it.

It's actually quite vexing especially given how irresistible it makes him look.

His eyes twinkle under the low light in the back of the Starbucks.

"I'm going as her plus one," I announce.

I make my voice extra perky on purpose.

So that it portrays excitement, rather than apprehensiveness, which is actually how I'm feeling over the whole thing.

"She's making you go as her plus one," Tom announces as a matter a fact. He knows me too well.

"I just don't get it, Ellie. I mean, why bother? It's a super yacht filled with filthy rich people. I mean, how fun can that party be?"

"Jealous much?" I ask.

"I'm not jealous at all!" He jumps back in his seat. "If that's what you think..."

He lets his words trail off and suddenly the conversation takes on a more serious mood.

"You don't have to worry, I'm not going to miss your engagement party," I say quietly. It's the weekend after I get back."

He shakes his head and insists that that's not what he's worried about.

"I just don't get it Ellie," he says.

You don't get it?

You don't get why I'm going?

I've had feelings for you for, what, two years now?

But the time was never right.

At first, I was with my boyfriend and the night of our breakup, you decided to kiss me.

You totally caught me off guard.

And after that long painful breakup, I wasn't ready for a relationship.

And you, my best friend, you weren't really a rebound contender.

And then, just as I was about to tell you how I felt, you spend the night with Carrie.

Beautiful, wealthy, witty Carrie. Carrie Warrenhouse, the current editor of BuzzPost, the online magazine where we both work, and the daughter of Edward Warrenhouse, the owner of

BuzzPost.

Oh yeah, and on top of all that, you also started seeing her and then asked her to marry you.

And now you two are getting married on Valentine's Day.

And I'm really happy for you.

Really.

Truly.

The only problem is that I'm also in love with you.

And now, I don't know what the hell to do with all of this except get away from New York.

Even if it's just for a few days.

But of course, I can't say any of these things.

Especially the last part.

"This hasn't been the best summer," I say after a few moments. "And I just want to do something fun. Get out of town. Go to a party. Because that's all this is, a party."

"That's not what I heard," Tom says.

"What do you mean?"

"Ever since you told me you were going, I started looking into this event.

And the rumor is that it's not what it is."

I shake my head, roll my eyes.

"What? You don't believe me?" Tom asks incredulously.

I shake my head.

"Okay, what? What did you hear?"

"It's basically like a Playboy Mansion party on steroids. It's totally out of control. Like one big orgy."

"And you would know what a Playboy Mansion party is like," I joke.

"I'm being serious, Ellie. I'm not sure this is a good place for you. I mean, you're not Caroline."

"And what the hell does that mean?" I ask.

Now, I'm actually insulted.

At first, I was just listening because I thought he was being protective.

But now...

"What you don't think I'm fun enough? You don't think I like to have a good time?" I ask.

"That's not what I meant," Tom backtracks. I start to gather my stuff. "What are you doing?"

"No, you know what," I stop packing up my stuff. "I'm not leaving. You're leaving."

"Why?"

"Because I came here to write. I have work to do. I staked out this table and I'm not leaving until I have

281

something written. I thought you wanted to have coffee with me. I thought we were friends. I didn't realize that you came here to chastise me about my decisions."

"That's not what I'm doing," Tom says, without getting out of his chair.

"You have to leave Tom. I want you to leave."

"I just don't understand what happened to us," he says getting up, reluctantly.

I stare at him as if he has lost his mind.

"You have no right to tell me what I can or can't do. You don't even have the right to tell your fiancée. Unless you don't want her to stay your fiancée for long."

"I'm not trying to tell you what to do, Ellie. I'm just worried. This super exclusive party on some mega-yacht, that's not you. That's not us."

"Not us? You've got to be kidding," I shake my head. "You graduated from Princeton, Tom. Your father is an attorney at one of the most prestigious law-firms in Boston. He has argued cases before the Supreme Court. You're going to marry the heir to the Warrenhouse fortune. I'm so sick and tired of your working class hero attitude, I can't even tell you. Now, are you going to leave or should I?"

The disappointment that I saw in Tom's eyes hurt me to my very soul.

But he had hurt me.

His engagement came completely out of left field.

I had asked him to give me some time after my breakup and after waiting for only two months, he started dating Carrie.

And then they moved in together. And then he asked her to marry him.

And throughout all that, he just sort of pretended that we were still friends.

Just like none of this ever happened.

I open my computer and stare at the half written story before me.

Earlier today, before Caroline, before Tom, I had all of these ideas.

I just couldn't wait to get started.

But now...I doubted that I could even spell my name right.

Staring at a non-moving blinker never fuels the writing juices.

I close my computer and look around the place.

All around me, people are laughing and talking.

Leggings and Uggs are back in season – even though the days are still warm and crispy.

It hasn't rained in close to a week and everyone's

good mood seems to be energized by the bright rays of the afternoon sun.

Last spring, I was certain that Tom and I would get together over the summer and I would spend the fall falling in love with my best friend.

And now?

Now, he's engaged to someone else.

Not just someone else – my boss!

And we just had a fight over some stupid party that I don't even really want to go to.

He's right, of course.

It's not my style.

My family might have money, but that's not the world in which I'm comfortable.

I'm always standing on the sidelines and it's not going to be any different at this party.

But if I don't go now, after this, that means that I'm listening to him.

And he has no right to tell me what to do.

So, I have to go.

How did everything get so messed up?

CHAPTER 3 - ELLIE

WHEN YOU GO SHOPPING FOR THE
PARTY OF A LIFETIME...

"What the hell are you still doing hanging out with that asshole?" Caroline asks dismissively.

We are in Elle's, a small boutique in Soho, where you can shop by appointment only.

I didn't even know these places existed until Caroline introduced me to the concept.

Caroline is not a fan of Tom.

They never got along, not since he called her an East Side snob at our junior year Christmas party at Yale and she called him a middle class poseur.

Neither insult was very creative, but their insults got better over the years as their hatred for each other grew.

You know how in the movies, two characters who

hate each other in the beginning always end up falling in love by the end?

Well, for a while, I actually thought that would happen to them.

If not fall in love, at least hook up. But no, they stayed steadfast in their hatred.

"That guy is such a tool. I mean, who the hell is he to tell you what to do anyway? It's not like you're his girlfriend," Caroline says placing a silver beaded bandage dress to her body and extending her right leg in front.

Caroline is definitely a knock out.

She's 5'10", 125 pounds with legs that go up to her chin.

In fact, from far away, she seems to be all blonde hair and legs and nothing else.

"I think he was just concerned, given all the stuff that is out there about this party."

"Okay, first of all, you have to stop calling it a party."

"Why? What is it?"

"It's not a party. It's like calling a wedding a party. Is it a party? Yes. But is it bigger than that."

"I had no idea that you were so sensitive to language. Fine. What do you want me to call it?'

"An experience," she announces, completely seriously.

"Are you kidding me? No way. There's no way I'm going to call it an experience."

We browse in silence for a few moments.

Some of the dresses and tops and shoes are pretty, some aren't.

I'm the first to admit that I do not have the vocabulary or knowledge to appreciate a place like this.

Now, Caroline on the other hand...

"Oh my God, I'm just in love with all these one of a kind pieces you have here," she says to the woman upfront who immediately starts to beam with pride.

"That's what we're going for."

"These statement bags and the detailing on these booties – agh! To die for, right?" Caroline says and they both turn to me.

"Yeah, totally," I agree blindly.

"And these high-end core pieces, I could just wear this every day!" Caroline pulls up a rather structured cream colored short sleeve shirt with a tassel hem and a boxy fit.

I'm not sure what makes that shirt a so-called core piece, but I go with the flow.

I'm out of my element and I know it.

"Okay, so what are we supposed to wear to this *experience* if we don't even know what's going to be going on there."

"I'm not exactly sure but definitely not jeans and t-shirts," Caroline says referring to my staple outfit. "But the invitation also said not to worry. They have all the necessities if we forget something."

As I continue to aimlessly browse, my mind starts to wander.

And goes back to Tom.

I met Tom at the Harvard-Yale game.

He was my roommate's boyfriend's high school best friend and he came up for the weekend to visit him.

We became friends immediately.

One smile from him, even on Skype, made all of my worries disappear.

He just sort of got me, the way no one really did.

After graduation, we applied to work a million different online magazines and news outlets, but BuzzPost was the one place that took both of us.

We didn't exactly plan to end up at the same place, but it was a nice coincidence.

He even asked if I wanted to be his roommate – but I had already agreed to room with Caroline.

He ended up in this crappy fourth floor walkup

in Hell's Kitchen – one of the only buildings that they haven't gentrified yet.

So, the rent was still somewhat affordable. Like I said, Tom likes to think of himself as a working class hero even though his upbringing is far from it.

Whenever he came over to our place, he always made fun of how expensive the place was, but it was always in good fun.

At least, it felt like it at the time.

Now?

I'm not so sure anymore.

"Do you think that Tom is really going to get married?" I ask Caroline while we're changing.

She swings my curtain open in front of the whole store.

I'm topless, but luckily I'm facing away from her and the assistant is buried in her phone.

"What are you doing?" I shriek and pull the curtain closed.

"What are you thinking?" she demands.

I manage to grab a shirt and cover myself before Caroline pulls the curtain open again.

She is standing before me in only a bra and a matching pair of panties – completely confident and unapologetic.

I think she's my spirit animal.

"Who cares about Tom?" Caroline demands.

"I do," I say meekly.

"Well, you shouldn't. He's a dick. You are way too good for him. I don't even understand what you see in him."

"He's my friend," I say as if that explains everything.

Caroline knows how long I've been in love with Tom.

She knows everything.

At times, I wish I hadn't been so open.

But other times, it's nice to have someone to talk to.

Even if she isn't exactly understanding.

"You can't just go around pining for him, Ellie. You can do so much better than him. You were with your ex and he just hung around waiting and waiting. Never telling you how he felt. Never making any grand gestures."

Caroline is big on gestures.

The grander the better.

She watches a lot of movies and she demands them of her dates.

And the funny thing is that you often get exactly what you ask from the world.

"I don't care about that," I say. "We were in the wrong place for each other.

I was with someone and then I wasn't ready to jump into another relationship right away.

And then...he and Carrie got together."

"There's no such thing as not the right time. Life is what you make it, Ellie. You're in control of your life. And I hate the fact that you're acting like you're not the main character in your own movie."

"I don't even know what you're talking about," I say.

"All I'm saying is that you deserve someone who tells you how he feels. Someone who isn't afraid of rejection. Someone who isn't afraid to put it all out there."

"Maybe that's who you want," I say.

"And that's not who you want?" Caroline says taking a step back away from me.

I think about it for a moment.

"Well, no I wouldn't say that. It is who I want," I finally say. "But I had a boyfriend then. And Tom and I were friends. So I couldn't expect him to—"

"You couldn't expect him to put it all out there? Tell you how he feels and take the risk of getting hurt?" Caroline cuts me off.

I hate to admit it, but that's exactly what I want.

That's exactly what I wanted from him back then.

I didn't want him to just hang around being my friend, making me question my feelings for him.

And if he had done that, if he had told me how he felt about me earlier, before my awful breakup, then I would've jumped in.

I would've broken up with my ex immediately to be with him.

"So, is that what I should do now? Now that things are sort of reversed?" I ask.

"What do you mean?"

"I mean, now that he's the one in the relationship. Should I just put it all out there? Tell him how I feel. Leave it all on the table, so to speak."

Caroline takes a moment to think about this.

I appreciate it because I know how little she thinks of him.

"Because I don't know if I can," I add quietly.

"Maybe that's your answer right there," Caroline finally says. "If you did want him, really want him to be yours, then you wouldn't be able to not to. You'd have to tell him."

I go back into my dressing room and pull the curtain closed.

I look at myself in the mirror.

The pale girl with green eyes and long dark hair is a coward.

She is afraid of life.

Afraid to really live.

Would this ever change?

CHAPTER 4 - ELLIE

WHEN YOU DECIDE TO LIVE
YOUR LIFE...

"*A*re you ready?" Caroline bursts into my room. "Our cab is downstairs."

No, I'm not ready.

Not at all.

But I'm going.

I take one last look in the mirror and grab my suitcase.

As the cab driver loads our bags into the trunk, Caroline takes my hand, giddy with excitement.

Excited is not how I would describe my state of being.

More like reluctant.

And terrified.

When I get into the cab, my stomach drops and I feel like I'm going to throw up.

But then the feeling passes.

"I can't believe this is actually happening," I say.

"I know, right? I'm so happy you're doing this with me, Ellie. I mean, really. I don't know if I could go by myself."

After ten minutes of meandering through the convoluted streets of lower Manhattan, the cab drops us off in front of a nondescript office building.

"Is the party here?" I ask.

Caroline shakes her head with a little smile on her face.

She knows something I don't know.

I can tell by that mischievous look on her face.

"What's going on?" I ask.

But she doesn't give in.

Instead, she just nudges me inside toward the security guard at the front desk.

She hands him a card, he nods, and shows us to the elevator.

"Top floor," he says.

When we reach the top floor, the elevator doors swing open on the roof and a strong gust of wind knocks into me.

Out of the corner of my eye, I see it.

The helicopter.

The blades are already going.

A man approaches us and takes our bags.

"What are we doing here?" I yell on top of my lungs.

But Caroline doesn't hear me.

I follow her inside the helicopter, ducking my head to make sure that I get in all in one piece.

A few minutes later, we take off.

We fly high above Manhattan, maneuvering past the buildings as if we're birds.

I've never been in a helicopter before and, a part of me, wishes that I'd had some time to process this beforehand.

"I didn't tell you because I thought you would freak," Caroline says into her headset.

She knows me too well.

She pulls out her phone and we pose for a few selfies.

"It's beautiful up here," I say looking out the window.

In the afternoon sun, the Manhattan skyline is breathtaking.

The yellowish red glow bounces off the glass buildings and shimmers in the twilight.

I don't know where we are going, but for the first time in a long time, I don't care.

I stay in the moment and enjoy it for everything it's worth.

Quickly the skyscrapers and the endless parade of bridges disappear and all that remains below us is the glistening of the deep blue sea.

And then suddenly, somewhere in the distance I see it.

The yacht.

At first, it appears as barely a speck on the horizon.

But as we fly closer, it grows in size.

By the time we land, it seems to be the size of its own island.

* * *

A TALL, beautiful woman waves to us as we get off the helicopter.

She's holding a plate with glasses of champagne and nods to a man in a tuxedo next to her to take our bags.

"Wow, that was quite an entrance," Caroline says to me.

"Mr. Black knows how to welcome his guests," the woman says. "My name is Lizbeth and I am here to serve you."

Lizbeth shows us around the yacht and to our stateroom.

"There will be cocktails right outside when you're ready," Lizbeth said before leaving us alone.

As soon as she left, we grabbed hands and let out a big yelp.

"Oh my God! Can you believe this place?" Caroline asks.

"No, it's amazing," I say, running over to the balcony. The blueness of the ocean stretched out as far as the eye could see.

"Are you going to change for cocktails?" Caroline asks, sitting down at the vanity. "The helicopter did a number on my hair."

We both crack up laughing.

Neither of us have ever been on a helicopter before – let alone a boat this big.

I decide against a change of clothes – my Nordstrom leggings and polka dot blouse should do just fine for cocktail hour.

But I do slip off my pair of flats and put on a nice pair of pumps, to dress up the outfit a little bit.

While Caroline changes into her short black dress, I brush the tangles out of my hair and reapply my lipstick.

"Ready?" Caroline asks.

Can't wait to read more? **One-Click BLACK EDGE Now!**

ABOUT CHARLOTTE BYRD

Charlotte Byrd is the bestselling author of many contemporary romance novels. She lives in Southern California with her husband, son, and a crazy toy Australian Shepherd. She loves books, hot weather and crystal blue waters.

Write her here:
charlotte@charlotte-byrd.com
Check out her books here:
www.charlotte-byrd.com
Connect with her here:
www.facebook.com/charlottebyrdbooks
Instagram: @charlottebyrdbooks
Twitter: @ByrdAuthor
Facebook Group: Charlotte Byrd's Reader Club
Newsletter